Francis Richard Charles Grant

Life of Samuel Johnson

Francis Richard Charles Grant

Life of Samuel Johnson

ISBN/EAN: 9783337055424

Printed in Europe, USA, Canada, Australia, Japan

Cover: Foto ©Raphael Reischuk / pixelio.de

More available books at **www.hansebooks.com**

OF

SAMUEL JOHNSON

BY

LIEUT.-COL. F. GRANT

-

LONDON
WALTER SCOTT
24 WARWICK LANE, PATERNOSTER ROW
1887

CONTENTS.

CHAPTER I.

CHAPTER II.

CHAPTER III.

CHAPTER IV.

CHAPTER V.

CHAPTER VI.

CHAPTER VII.

CHAPTER VIII.

CHAPTER IX.

CONTENTS.

LIFE OF JOHNSON.

—◆—

CHAPTER I.

IN the parish register of Packwood, in Warwickshire is the following entry :—

> *MICKELL JOHNSONES, of lichfield and* ⎫ 1706.
> *SARA FORD maried June y^e 19th,* ⎭

The bridegroom, Michael Johnson, a bookseller of good repute, was fifty years of age, and the bride thirty-seven. It was more than three years after this marriage that their eldest child was born at Lichfield on the 18th of September, 1709. He was named Samuel after a maternal uncle, Samuel Ford, or perhaps after his godfather, Dr. Samuel Swinfen, who, at that time, was lodging with the family at the old house in the market-place, opposite St. Mary's Church. Dr. Swinfen, a gentleman of ancient family, who had property in the neighbourhood, and latterly acquired some eminence as a physician, took a warm interest in his godson's career, and it may have been, partly through his advice and encouragement, that the lad was in due course sent to Oxford, where he entered at Pembroke, Dr. Swinfen's own college. This kindness was repaid in after days, when Dr. Swinfen's daughter, Mrs. Desmoulins, was received into Johnson's house, and found a home there until the death of her host. Of Michael Johnson's second son, Nathaniel, little is known. He was about three years younger than Samuel, who, according to Mrs. Thrale, spoke with pride of his younger brother's manly spirit and powers of endurance. After the death of his father, Nathaniel looked after the business, but his life was comparatively short. He died in his twenty-fifth year.

Young Samuel Johnson was afflicted with the hereditary disease, known as the "king's evil," and, in accordance with the custom of that age, his mother took him to London, in 1712, when he was three years old, to be touched by the Queen, who, with the form of prayer, used on those occasions, placed round his neck an "angel of gold noble," with St. Michael on the one side, and on the reverse a ship under full sail. It is supposed that this was the last time that the quaint service "for the healing," [1] which may be found in the Common Prayer Books of Queen Anne's reign, was performed in this country. Some of the incidents of the journey to London are recorded in his fragment of an autobiography, published in 1805, and, in connection with the ceremony, Johnson throughout his life retained "a confused, but somehow a solemn, recollection of a lady in diamonds and a long black hood."

---

[1] In 1686, by order of James II., were published "The Ceremonies for the Healing of them that be Diseased with the King's Evil," and also the "Office of Consecrating Cramp Rings."

But the more practical business of life was now to commence, and the future author of the English dictionary was sent to a school kept by Dame Oliver in Dam Street, at the north corner of Quonian's Lane. Both these places, which have retained their original names, are still (1887) in existence, and the schoolroom with the Dame's residence attached, and the boys' playing ground on the opposite side of the lane, are easily identified. This curious relic of old Lichfield, which must have been an ancient building, even in Johnson's schooldays, seems hitherto to have escaped notice. The schoolmistress declared that Johnson was the best scholar she ever had, and when, some years later, he was leaving Lichfield to begin his career at Oxford, she brought him a present of gingerbread. "This," said Johnson, "was as high a proof of merit as he could conceive." Perhaps in after days he was reminded of the incident, when reading the lines in Shenstone's "Schoolmistress"—

> " And to the well-known Chest the Dame repair,
>   Whence oft with sugar'd Cates she doth them greet,
>   And Gingerbread y—rare." . . . .

After leaving Dame Oliver, the lad was placed under charge of a master, of whom his pupil's chief recollection was that he published a spelling-book, and dedicated it to the universe. What a prize this little volume would now be for an enthusiastic book hunter ! After learning all that could be taught by Tom Brown, the author of the spelling-book, he was sent to the Lichfield Grammar School, then under Mr. Hunter, a severe disciplinarian, who is said to have been " an odd mixture of the pedant and the sportsman," and who forgave any offence to a boy, who would tell him where to find a covey of partridges. Johnson always remembered his master's severity, and in his old age used to say, half humorously, that he could never see Miss Seward, who bore a strong resemblance to her grandfather, Mr. Hunter, without a feeling of awe. The place, however, had a good reputation, and at one period there were five judges on the bench, who had been brought up at the Lichfield Grammar School. But there was a still more interesting record in its history. It was there, immediately before going to the Charterhouse, that Addison received a portion of his education, and Johnson states in his biography that he was the leader in a " barring out."

Among Johnson's schoolfellows were some whose friendship he retained throughout life. In his own form was Charles Congreve, who was afterwards chaplain to Archbishop Boulter, Swift's powerful adversary in Dublin. Congreve, in later years, became a confirmed valetudinarian, and in 1776, was living in London, looked after by an elderly woman, whom he called cousin. She encouraged him in drinking, in which he was very willing to be encouraged, and he had become " quite unsocial," and his conversation was " quite monosyllabic." When Johnson, at the last recorded visit, asked him what o'clock it was, that signal of departure " had so pleasing an effect on him that he sprang up to look at his watch like a greyhound bounding at a hare."

But of all the Lichfield boys, Johnson in after life was most intimate with Dr. John Taylor, and Mr. Edmund Hector. With the former, who subsequently became pre-

bendary of Westminster, he maintained to the end a
constant and friendly intercourse, and was frequently a
visitor at his patrimonial estate at Ashbourne. On the
death of Mrs. Johnson, he sent off immediately to Dr.
Taylor, who hastened to the summons, and did all that
was possible to calm his friend's violent grief. Next day
Johnson wrote again: "Let me have your company
and instruction. Do not live away from me; my distress is great." When the year before his death, he was
struck with palsy, he wrote at once to Taylor: "Let me
see you as soon as possible;" and again on his death-
bed it was his old friend and schoolfellow, who read
prayers to the dying man, and afterwards performed the
funeral service over his grave in the Abbey.

Most of our knowledge of Johnson's school life is
derived from Edmund Hector, who appears to have been
the chosen companion of his early days. The two lads
used, in their play hours, to saunter about the fields round
Lichfield, and Hector was never tired of telling of his
friend's moral influence with his comrades, and how the
boys used to call at his house every morning, and carry
him to school on their shoulders. But it has been
shrewdly suggested that this ascendency was as much due
to Johnson's strength and courage as to his intellectual
superiority. Hector settled down in due course as a
surgeon in Birmingham, and Johnson was always delighted when he had an opportunity of seeing his old
friend, whose sister, he told Boswell, was the first woman
he ever loved. To this object of his early admiration he
sent an affectionate message in a letter, written shortly
before his death. Mr. Hector, who was about the same

age as his friend, survived him nearly ten years, and died in 1794.

Boswell mentions Dr. James, the inventor of the fever powder, as another of Johnson's schoolfellows, but this statement appears open to question, as James was his senior by eight years; they were, without doubt, however, on intimate terms, and, according to Mrs. Thrale, James knew the history of his friend's early days better than any one. It was probably by him that Johnson was introduced to John Newbery, the publisher, at whose house he must first have met Oliver Goldsmith. Another Lichfield schoolfellow, Lowe, had the reputation, among the boys, of being the only pupil who was as good a scholar as Johnson. Lowe took orders, and eventually became a Canon of Windsor. Of a Joseph Simpson we hear something, through a casual mention by Johnson, half a century later. He was a barrister, and not wanting in ability, but fell into a dissipated life, and lost his practice. A tragedy from his pen, called "The Patriot," [1] was published as the work of Johnson the year after its author's death. Mr. Jackson, a schoolfellow, whose career was not more successful than Simpson's, dined with Johnson and Boswell at the inn, at Lichfield, in 1776, and "seemed to be a low man, dull and untaught. He had a coarse gray coat, black waistcoat, greasy leather breeches, and a yellow, uncurled wig; and his countenance had the ruddiness which betokens one who is in no haste to 'leave his can.' He drank only ale. He had tried to be a cutler at

[1] "'The Patriot :' a Tragedy. From a Manuscript of the late Dr. Johnson, corrected by himself. London, 1765."

Birmingham, but had not succeeded; and now he lived poorly at home, and had some scheme of dressing leather in a better manner than common."

After leaving Lichfield Grammar School, Johnson spent some time with his relative, Cornelius Ford. It has been doubted if this were an uncle or cousin of Johnson. Mr. Napier, in a note to his edition of Boswell's "Life," has shown that there were two persons of this name, the one a brother, the other a nephew of Johnson's mother. The latter was a clergyman of excellent abilities, but of profligate life, and it is supposed, with some authority, that he was the original of the parson in Hogarth's Midnight Modern Conversation, but it was more likely intended for Orator Henley, who appears in another of the artist's well-known caricatures. It was to his uncle that the boy was now sent to continue his studies, and he remained there till he was fifteen. After an attempt to be received as scholar and usher at Newport, in Shropshire, he went to Stourbridge school, then under the charge of a Mr. Wentworth, an able man, from whom his pupil confessed to have learnt a great deal. He appears to have mixed in society at Stourbridge more than was usual for a boy of his age, and to have passed some of his leisure hours in writing verses to the young ladies in the neighbourhood. With one of these, Olivia Lloyd, he imagined himself to be seriously in love. She was a Quaker, and probably belonged to the same family as Mr. Lloyd, whom Boswell met, when on a visit with Johnson to Birmingham, in 1776. He was at Stourbridge for about a year, and then returned to his father's house, where he remained till he went to Oxford,

and, during this time, he no doubt got through a good
deal of desultory reading. On one occasion he relates
that, in looking for apples in a loft, he came across a
folio of Petrarch, and read through a great part of the
book. He afterwards said, in allusion to his course of
reading at that time: "I had looked into a great many
books that were not commonly known at the university,
. . . so that when I came to Oxford, Dr. Adams, now
master of Pembroke College, told me I was the best
qualified for the university that he had ever known come
there." During the two years spent at home, he probably helped in his father's shop, and Hawkins asserts
that he used to say that he was able to bind a book.
Michael Johnson was accustomed to open a stall on
market days in some of the neighbouring towns, and it
was perhaps about this time that the lad refused to attend
his father on one of these occasions to Uttoxeter market.
Many years later he went to the old town, and, in very
bad weather, remained, bareheaded, on the spot where his
father's stall used to be held. "In contrition I stood,"
he said, "and I hope the penance was expiatory."
This act of atonement has been commented on in
various ways, but it certainly shows a tender conscience;
and Carlyle once told Mr. Froude that he felt inclined
to do penance in a similar manner for some act which
troubled his mind.

When Johnson arrived at literary eminence, he was
famous, not only for his extensive reading, but also for
his knowledge of books. He could tell without hesitation
the names of the best authors on any particular subject,
and it seems probable that he partly acquired this know-

ledge from assisting in his father's business.   He must also have learnt a good deal in after days while engaged in cataloguing Lord Oxford's library for Osborne the bookseller.   Nothing was more remarkable than his minute acquaintance with obscure literature.   No one has ever yet been able to ascertain the source of the lines, which he repeated, on hearing a girl at Nairn singing over her spinning-wheel.

> " Verse sweetens toil, however rude the sound ;
>   All at her work the village maiden sings ;
>   Nor, while she turns the giddy wheel around,
>   Revolves the sad vicissitudes of things."

On one occasion, when driving with a friend at Brighton, he repeated with great precision three stanzas, afterwards found among some anonymous poems in a volume of Lintot's "Miscellanies."   At another time Miss Seward wished to know who had written some verses addressed to Pope, in one of the notes of "The Dunciad," and he was able immediately to name the author.

It was at length determined to send the boy to Oxford. Hawkins says that the step was taken on the understanding that he was to go to the university as tutor to Mr. Andrew Corbett, the son of a gentleman in the neighbourhood, who was *about* to send his son to Pembroke College ; but this cannot be entirely accurate, as Corbett's name appears on the books twenty months before Johnson was entered.   Another suggestion, which appears more probable, is that his expenses were to be defrayed by Mr. Swinfen and some other residents of Lichfield ; but in this case it is difficult to explain why this assistance should so soon have been stopped. Boswell, with more tact than he usually displayed, refrained from questioning his friend on the subject, about which it is, now, no longer possible to obtain any definite information.

CHAPTER II

A T the age of nineteen Samuel Johnson entered at Pembroke College on the 31st of October, 1728. An account of his first evening at the University was given by Dr. Adams, who was present on the occasion. His father accompanied him, and they were introduced to Mr. Jorden, who was appointed to be the lad's tutor. The new undergraduate's uncouth appearance caused some surprise, but he was modest and respectful, and for a time took no part in the conversation. At length, however, he could keep silence no longer, and joined in with a quotation from Macrobius, an author who was probably little known, except by name, to any other of the party. Those who wish to know something of life at Oxford in the early part of the last century should read the opening chapter in Dr. G. Birkbeck Hill's carefully written work, "Johnson, his Friends and his Critics," from which the present writer has derived much valuable information.

The University at that time offered few of the advantages which its members now enjoy. There were no inducements for the undergraduates to read, and, if they wished to do so, it was only in a few colleges that the tutors' lectures were worth attending. A degree was conferred, as a matter of course, after the requisite number of terms had been kept. "The one very powerful incentive to learning," writes Johnson, in one of his "Idlers," "is the genius of the place;" but it is not every undergraduate who would be inspired by this influence, and the want of good college tutors was felt long after the "Idler's" time. More than a century later, a raw Yorkshire youth, "incredibly raw," as he himself says, with an ardent thirst for knowledge, and destined afterwards to attain high academical distinction, was taken by his father to Oxford to begin his University career. It is interesting to contrast the account which Dr. Mark Pattison gave of his first impression of college life with Johnson's experience on a similar occasion, and it is not difficult to find certain points of resemblance. Soon after he arrived at Oxford, the young undergraduate, who had surprised his tutor by quoting Macrobius, was asked to show his abilities as a Latin poet by rendering Pope's "Messiah" into hexameters. The style of the translation is not Virgilian, though his friend, Mr. Thomas Warton, afterwards Professor of Poetry at Oxford, did not venture to tell him so when discussing the poem on a subsequent occasion, and got out of the difficulty by speaking of one of the lines as "very sonorous." Pope, to whom the translation was shown by a son of his old friend, Dr. Arbuthnot, declared that the "writer of this poem will leave it a question for posterity whether his or mine is the original." It afterwards appeared in a miscellany of poems, published at Oxford in 1731, and edited by Mr. John Husband, a contemporary of Johnson at Pembroke College. In the preface to the volume the editor writes: "The Translation of Mr. Pope's 'Messiah' was deliver'd to his Tutor, as a College Exercise, by Mr. Johnson, a Commoner of Pembroke College in Oxford, and 'tis hoped will be no discredit to the excellent Original." But perhaps the most curious part of the work is the circumstance, hitherto unnoticed, that among the list of subscribers appears the name of Richard Savage for twenty copies. This piece of extravagance is very characteristic of that eccentric creature, but it is not easy to explain, unless it was a compliment to Johnson, with whom he was afterwards on terms of great intimacy. This strange friendship, however, is not supposed to have commenced till some years later, but any attempts to solve the difficulty would necessarily be mere guess work.

The duration of Johnson's college career has given rise to much controversy, though there is no part of his life which ought to be better known. Dr. Adams, who was a fellow of Pembroke College when Johnson first entered, and Taylor, another Oxford contemporary, though at a different college, were both well acquainted with Boswell, and furnished him with particulars for the "Life." Boswell asserted that Johnson was at Oxford for about three years, and Hawkins, whose biography had previously been published, gave practically the same account. Boswell's accuracy has been so often proved, and his opportunities of obtaining information on the subject were so exceptional, that it is difficult not to accept his statement ; but Croker, from an inspection of the college books, showed, almost beyond a doubt, that Johnson could not have been in residence for more than fourteen months. The difficulty, in this view of the case, was to account for the fact that Johnson himself spoke of his college intercourse with Taylor, who matriculated on June 27, 1730, nearly six months after Johnson (if Croker's view is correct) had left the University. This discrepancy has now been satisfactorily explained by Dr. George Birkbeck Hill, who discovered in the Christ Church books the names of two John Taylors, one of whom matriculated February 24, 1729, only four months after Johnson. Boswell, in this instance, therefore, seems to have been mistaken, and though Johnson's name does not finally disappear from the college books till October, 1731, he was an actual member for only fourteen months, and his residence virtually came to an end in December, 1729, when he made a note, "1729. Dec. S. J. Oxonio rediit."

Many stories have been told, some of them on Johnson's own authority, of his insubordination at college, but there is reason to think that remorse induced him to exaggerate his failings, and Boswell heard from Dr. Adams that he was a regular attendant at the college lectures.

Johnson had not many opportunities in after life of meeting his Oxford contemporaries, with the exception of Adams and Taylor. The latter has been already referred to, and Adams, who spoke of himself as Johnson's " nominal tutor," continued through life his constant and valued friend. He was one of those present on the first night of Johnson's tragedy of " Irene," and gave Boswell an account of that memorable occasion. When his old pupil first revisited Oxford, in 1754, he appears to have been absent, but after he became head of his college, in 1775, Johnson was several times a guest at the Master's

Lodge. Dr. Adams was also rector of St. Chad's, in Shrewsbury, where he received a visit from Johnson and the Thrales, during their Welsh tour in 1774. He survived his old college friend about four years, and died in 1789, aged eighty-two.

Of "Honest Jack Meeke of Pembroke College," as his name appears scribbled at the end of the college buttery books, there is little to be said, though Johnson was, in those days, very jealous of his superiority, and sat as far from him as possible at college lectures, so as not to hear him construe. Boswell gives an account, which he had from Mr. Warton, of a very cordial meeting between the former rivals, when Johnson was at Oxford in 1754. During a later visit to the University, in 1776, we hear of two other college companions, whose names, by this chance mention, have been rescued from oblivion. "Ah, here," said Johnson, in the Pembroke common room, "I used to play at draughts with Phil Jones and Fludyer. Jones loved beer, and did not get very forward in the Church. Fludyer turned out a scoundrel and a Whig, and said he was ashamed of having been bred at Oxford. He had a living at Putney, and got under the eye of some retainers of the Court at that time, and so became a violent Whig. . . ." Fludyer's change of politics was not of much service to him in obtaining preferment, as it appears from the parish registers that he remained perpetual curate of Putney till his death, which occurred in 1773.

One of the most interesting events in Johnson's life, though it did not happen till 1778, relates to his college career. He himself briefly mentions the incident in the "Prayers and Meditations;" but Boswell's account of the

affair is given with even more than his usual skill and
dramatic power.   On the way home from church on
Good Friday, Johnson, who was accompanied by Boswell,
met an old fellow collegian whom he had not seen since
they were undergraduates together in 1729.   "Mr.
Edwards, who was a decent-looking elderly man in grey
clothes and a wig of many curls, accosted him with
familiar confidence, knowing who he was, while Johnson
returned his salutation with a courteous formality as to a
stranger.   But as soon as Edwards had brought to his
recollection their having been at Pembroke College together nine and forty years ago, he seemed much pleased,
asked where he lived, and said he should be glad to see
him at Bolt Court."   Boswell whispered to Edwards that
the doctor was going home, and that he had better
accompany him.   On the way thither Edwards mentioned
that he had practised as a solicitor in Chancery, and that
he lived on a little farm in Hertfordshire.   The dialogue,
which ensued on arrival at Bolt Court, is a good example
of Boswell's reporting, but there is only space for some
extracts.   Johnson, who had been talking of the respon-
sibilities of a clergyman's life, exclaimed abruptly—

"Oh, Mr. Edwards, I'll convince you that I recollect
you.   Do you remember our drinking together at an alehouse near Pembroke Gate?   At that time you told me
of the Eton boy who, when verses on our Saviour's turning water into wine were prescribed as an exercise, brought
up a single line, which was highly admired—

"'Vidit et erubuit nympha pudica Deum,'

and I told you of another fine line in Camden's "Re-

mains," an eulogy upon one of our kings, who was succeeded by his son, a prince of equal merit—

    " ' Mira cano, sol occubuit ; nox nulla secuta est.' "

After some conversation on other subjects, Edwards
remarked, " You are a philosopher, Dr. Johnson. I have
tried, too, in my time to be a philosopher ; but, I don't
know how, cheerfulness was always breaking in." Boswell
mentions that Burke, Reynolds, and all the eminent men,
to whom he mentioned this speech, thought it an exquisite
trait of character. The conversation then turned upon
wine, which Johnson said he now never drank.

  " *Edwards.* Don't you eat supper, sir ?
  " *Johnson.* No, sir.
  " *Edwards.* For my part, now, I consider supper as a
turnpike, through which one must pass in order to go to
bed."

Edwards meeting Johnson again, some time after, spoke
of *The Rambler* as a very pretty book, which he heard his
friend had written, and its author, " unwilling that he
should leave the world in total darkness," sent him a copy
of the work. Johnson's love and reverence for Oxford
seemed to increase as he grew older, and, to the end of
his life, he loved to revisit his old University, where
he never appeared except in correct academical costume.

Pembroke College is much changed since those days.
The present library, where is preserved Johnson's desk,
on which he wrote a portion of the " Dictionary," was
in his days the hall. He would scarcely recognize the
Master's House, occupied by that " fine Jacobite fellow,"
Dr. Panting, when Johnson first knew it, and where he

was staying as a guest, a few months before his death.
The tower, also, has undergone many alterations, but the
rooms on the second floor, above the ancient gateway, are
much the same as when he lived there.   The window of
the bedroom looks on the old quadrangle, and in the
rooms on the floor below, is an oriel window, facing
north, placed by the college in honour of its former illustrious member.

After a brief appearance at Oxford in October, 1731
(the last as an undergraduate), he returned home and was
present at his father's death in December.   Michael
Johnson's affairs had latterly become embarrassed, and,
from MS. letters, preserved at Pembroke College, it
appears that his widow was left in great poverty.   She
still, however, was able to keep on the business, and,
until his death, was helped by her younger son.   An old
servant of the family, Catherine Chambers, too, probably
made herself useful in the shop, and, in later years, Lucy
Porter, Samuel Johnson's step-daughter, never failed to
assist on market days, or when there was any press of
business.

The position occupied by Michael Johnson had been
far above that of an ordinary country tradesman, and it
was, no doubt, improved by his marriage with a lady be-
longing to an old, though not a distinguished, county
family.   He had held several important offices at Lichfield;
first of junior bailiff, and afterwards of sheriff; and, in
1725, he served as chief magistrate of the city.   The only
bookseller in the place, and even in the neighbourhood,
he was largely patronized by the clergy, who, probably on
market days, found his shop a convenient place of resort.

Besides books and pamphlets, Michael Johnson, like the Newberys, and other old-fashioned booksellers, sold patent medicines, and Hungary water, that perfume so dear to our forefathers in the reign of good Queen Anne. He was also a publisher, and books, with his imprint on the title-page, are still met with on rare occasions. In 1716, Lord Gower's chaplain wrote, "Johnson, the Lichfield librarian, is now here; he propagates learning all over the diocese, and advanceth knowledge to its just height; all the clergy here are his pupils, and suck all they have from him."

Samuel Johnson, on the death of his father, succeeded to an inheritance of only twenty pounds, and his prospects were not brilliant. It was necessary he should do something for his living, and he naturally turned to literature for support.

It is necessary to say a few words about the Lichfield society at that time, a point on which there has been much misapprehension. A few years later, when Johnson went to seek his fortunes in London, he was no doubt intimate with many of the laureates of Grub Street, and was compelled by poverty to mix with companions, of whom he afterwards had strange stories to relate; but, during this period at Lichfield, he associated with the best families of the place.

Dr. Swinfen, his godfather, was still living. He was a welcome guest at the house of the Hon. Henry Hervey, then a cornet of dragoons, who had married Catherine, eldest sister of Sir Thomas Aston. Mrs. Garrick, the mother of David Garrick, afterwards the greatest actor on the English stage, was settled with her family at Lich-

field, during the absence of her husband on foreign
service.   Her "dear life," as she calls him in her letters,
remained with his regiment at Gibraltar till 1736, and,
after an absence of five years, came back only to pass a
few happy months, and then to die.   Other friends were
Mr. Levett, a gentleman of property in the county ; and
Gilbert Walmsley, who, a few years later, married Mrs.
Hervey's sister ; George, subsequently Lord Lyttelton,
Johnson's supposed rival in the good graces of Molly
Aston, was also, according to Percy, sometimes in the
neighbourhood ; Ashbourne, where Taylor lived, was not
far off, and there were the Hickmans (relatives of his
mother), the Meynells of Bradley, and other families,
where he occasionally visited.

There is some doubt as to when he first knew the
Astons.   Mr. Croker thinks the acquaintance could
hardly at this time have commenced, as he supposes it
was made through Gilbert Walmsley, who was not married to Magdalen Aston [1] till 1736.   But Johnson was
by that time himself married, and it is more probable that
he first met them at the house of their brother-in-law,
Henry Hervey, whose regiment arrived in Lichfield about
the end of 1732.   He had a great admiration for one of
the sisters, Molly Aston, who he said was "a beauty and
a scholar, a wit and a Whig," and he declared in after
years "she was the loveliest creature I ever saw."   When
the Thrales asked him what was the happiest period of
his life, he replied, "It was that year in which I spent
one whole evening with Molly Aston ; that, indeed, was

---

[1] Croker calls her Margaret Aston, but in Gilbert Walmsley's epitaph, on the tablet in Lichfield Cathedral, she is called Magdalen.

not happiness, it was rapture ; but the thought of it sweet-
ened many a year." With two other sisters of Mrs.
Hervey, Mrs. Elizabeth Aston, and Mrs. Gastrell, who
eventually settled at Lichfield, Johnson remained on intimate terms till his death. Molly Aston became the wife
of a Captain Brodie of the navy, but she does not appear
after her marriage to have met her old admirer.

There is a good deal of uncertainty about much of Johnson's life between 1731 and 1736. After several unsuccessful attempts to obtain a situation as usher, he at length
received an appointment to the school at Market Bosworth.
He made the journey there on foot, on the 16th of July,
1732, but he found the position so intolerable that his
stay was short, and he was once more without em-
ployment. It may have been about this time that an
incident occurred in Johnson's life, lately communicated to *Notes and Queries*,[1] which had hitherto escaped
notice. From the following letter, written by the Rev. J.
Addenbroke, afterwards Dean of Lichfield, to Mr. Whitby,
great-grandfather of Mr. Whitby, of Creswell Hall, near
Stafford, it appears that Johnson was at one time acting
as tutor in the Whitby family.

" I have sent you enclosed Mr. Johnson's letter to Mr.
Levett. The sum I mentioned to Mr. Levett was as
little as, I thought, could be offered to a Gentleman of
Character for half-a-year's attendance. But his affairs, you
see, won't give him leave to be with your son so long. So
that if you'll let me know what will be agreeable to you
to give for that time, I'll communicate it to Mr. Levett,

[1] Nov. 29, 1884.

and the Gentleman may wait upon you immediately.   I
can only say, that if Mr. Johnson will do what He is
capable of doing in that time, He will be of more service
to your son than a year spent in the usual way at the
University.   I shall be glad to know your Resolution to
morrow; because I am obliged to go to Sudbury on
Monday, where I shall stay all the week.

<blockquote>
"I am, Sir,

"Your most Obed' Serv',

"J. ADDENBROKE.
</blockquote>

<blockquote>
" My humble service waite upon the Family.

"STAFFORD, *May* 10th."
</blockquote>

(s.d. but probably 1732, or 1733.)

There is a superscription written in 1824, by a Mr.
Thomas Whitby, grandson of the gentleman to whom the
letter is addressed :

<blockquote>
"CRESWELL, *Nov.* 18, 1824.
</blockquote>

" This letter (*i.e.* Mr. A.'s) was written probably to my
grandfather soon after Mr. Johnson (left?) Bosworth.   I
have frequently heard Mrs. Wells, my father's youngest
sister, say, that she remembered Mr. (Dr.) Johnson being
at Heywood as Tutor to her brother, and that he frequently
instructed her in the English language.

<blockquote>
"THOS. WHITBY."
</blockquote>

According to this, Johnson passed some time at Heywood, after he left Market Bosworth, but the matter is not

quite clear. It must have been shortly afterwards that he spent six months at Birmingham with his old schoolfellow, Hector, who was lodging "over against the Swan Tavern in High Street," [1] with Thomas Warren, the first book-seller established in Birmingham. Warren gave him some literary work, and he received five guineas to translate M. le Grand's French abridgment of Father Lobo's "Voyage to Abyssinia," which he borrowed from the library of Pembroke College. The Portuguese missionary, who relates that he saw several unicorns, can hardly be considered a trustworthy historian, but, as an early book of travels, it has a certain value, and some of M. le Grand's dissertations, especially that on the Queen of Sheba, are interesting. The English translator's preface, as Burke pointed out to Boswell, contains passages in decided Johnsonian style, but the "Voyage" itself is written in fluent English, free from all Gallicisms, and the reader will find no indication, from the first page to the last, that it is translated from a foreign language.

Johnson's natural indolence had already begun to assert itself, and a large portion of the MS. was written by Mr. Hector, while the translator dictated from his bed, and without this help, the work would probably have been abandoned. In 1734 he appears to have wandered between Lichfield and Birmingham, and from the latter place he wrote in November to Mr. Edward Cave, the editor of *The Gentleman's Magazine*, offering to supply literary articles. According to Haw-

[1] "Probably in one of the old half-timbered houses, pulled down when the railway tunnel was made in 1850."—Mr. Saml. Timmins' "Johnson in Birmingham."

kins a favourable answer was sent, but it is not known if
Johnson became at that time a contributor.

In 1735, Mr. Walmsley applied on Johnson's behalf
for the mastership of Solihull Grammar School. The
reply to the application is so curious that it is worth
quoting. The trustees, writes Mr. Greswold, obtained
satisfactory information as to Johnson's scholarship; " but
then," the letter goes on to say, "he has the character of
being a very haughty, ill-natured gent, and y^t he has such
a way of distorting his face (w^h though he can't help), y^e
gent think it may affect some young lads. . . ." A previous attempt to obtain the post of assistant, at a school
in Brewood, had failed for the same reasons.

But he was now about to enter into an engagement
of a more interesting character. While living with Mr.
Hector at Birmingham, he had made the acquaintance
of Mr. Porter (a mercer) and his wife. About this time
Mr. Porter died, and Johnson, who was one of the executors, became a candidate for the widow's hand. One
biographer says that it was the lady who made the first
advances, but, in any case, the affair was soon brought to
a successful issue, and the marriage took place at Derby
on July 9, 1735.

Boswell gives a curious account of the wedding, which
he heard from Johnson himself, who, though he had not
then edited Shakespeare's plays, was apparently well
acquainted with "The Taming of the Shrew!" "Sir,
she had read the old romances, and had got into her
head the fantastical notion that a woman of spirit should
use her lover like a dog. So, sir, at first she told me
that I rode too fast, and she could not keep up with me;

and, when I rode a little slower, she passed me, and complained that I lagged behind. I was not to be made the slave of caprice; and I resolved to begin as I meant to end. I therefore pushed on briskly till I was fairly out of her sight. The road lay between two hedges, so I was sure she could not miss it, and I contrived that she should soon come up with me; when she did, I observed her to be in tears." This "pretty charmer," as her husband sometimes called her, is thus described by Garrick: "She was very fat, with a bosom of more than ordinary protuberance; her swelled cheeks were of a florid red, produced by thick painting, and increased by the liberal use of cordials; flaring and fantastic in her dress, and affected both in her speech and general behaviour." This is probably somewhat exaggerated; and, in any case there is an engraving, now extremely rare, of her as a young woman, which represents a tolerably good-looking person. Of the bridegroom, his step-daughter, Lucy Porter, told Boswell that "his appearance was very forbidding: he was then lean and lanky, so that his immense structure of bone was hideously striking to the eye, and the scars of scrofula were deeply visible. He also wore his hair, which was straight and stiff, separated behind; and he often had seemingly convulsive starts and odd gesticulations, which tended to excite at once surprise and ridicule." The bride was in her forty-seventh year; the bridegroom was not quite twenty-six. He told his friend Beauclerk, with much gravity, "Sir, it was a love match on both sides." On one occasion, when they were walking together, a gipsy examined his hand, and told him his heart was divided between a

Molly and a Betty, but that though Betty loved him the best, he took most delight in Molly's company. "When I turned about to laugh," he said, in telling the story, "I saw my wife was crying. Pretty charmer, she had no reason." Mrs. Johnson's name was Elizabeth, and she knew of her husband's admiration for Molly Aston. As far as can be ascertained, the marriage was a happy one, and in after days he spoke of his wife with fond regret. When talking of her to Mrs. Thrale, he had nothing to complain of but her "particular reverence for cleanliness," which seems to have caused a good deal of annoyance to her husband.

But, without doubt, she was a woman of good understanding, and had a thorough appreciation of her husband's worth. To the last he thought her a beauty, and this may, to some extent, be explained by his imperfect vision, which toned down her high colour and exuberant proportions. Apart, however, from his admiration for her personal charms, his affection for her was very deep and earnest, and in the "Prayers and Meditations" her name is often mentioned with affection.

Johnson obtained with his wife a fortune of £800, but it appears from a deed, recently discovered, that a part of this was lost through the insolvency of a Birmingham attorney, named Perks. With the remainder the newly-married pair resolved to set up a school, and Edial Hall, near Lichfield, was hired for the undertaking. But, notwithstanding the exertions of friends, and advertisements in *The Gentleman's Magazine*, the academy never became a success. David Garrick and (according to Percy) Hawkesworth, both of them nearly arrived at man's estate, with George Garrick, a younger brother of David, were among the pupils, but the number never, at most, exceeded eight. After about a year and a half the school was given up, and Johnson determined to seek his fortunes in London.

CHAPTER III.

WHILE Johnson was at Edial Hall he had commenced his tragedy of "Irene," founded on an incident in Knolles's "History of the Turks." He had shown this production to his friend Gilbert Walmsley, Registrar of the Ecclesiastical Court, who pointed out that the misfortunes of the heroine had begun too early in the play. "How can you possibly contrive," he said, "to plunge her into deeper calamity?" "Sir," said Dr. Johnson, "I can put her into the Spiritual Court." Mr. Walmsley, however, notwithstanding the premature sorrows of Irene, thought well of the piece, and advised its author to finish it. With this tragedy, of which only the first three acts were then written, Johnson started for London, without any fixed plan, except to finish "Irene," and to get it produced on the stage.

He had probably selected the branch of literature in which he was least qualified to succeed, but the theatre in those days offered great attractions to literary men. It undoubtedly appeared the easiest road to fame and fortune, and the works of writers, little conversant with the drama, had achieved brilliant success on the stage. Addison's "Cato" had been received with unbounded applause by the public, and the play, when published, had gone through eight editions in less than six months. For the "Conscious Lovers," Steele, besides the customary profits, which must have been considerable, received a present of five hundred guineas from the king. The "Beggar's Opera" had won a popularity such as no play by Congreve or Farquhar had ever obtained, and Gay received for his share of the "author's nights" about seven hundred pounds. It can scarcely be thought surprising that a novice, about to plunge into the struggles of literary life, should turn his eyes to the theatre, where it was possible to obtain such profitable results.

Johnson was accompanied to London by his old pupil, David Garrick, who was intended to read for the Bar, but of this interesting journey we have no satisfactory account, though there is one humorous story on the subject. "That was the year," said Johnson, at a large dinner party, by way of fixing the date of some event, "when I came to London with twopence-halfpenny in my pocket." Garrick, who was present, overhearing him, exclaimed : "Eh ! what do you say ? with twopence-halfpenny in your pocket ? " "Why, yes," replied Johnson, "when I came with twopence-halfpenny in my pocket, and thou, Davy, with three-halfpence in thine." Garrick, who could have supplied Boswell with valuable information on this and other subjects, connected with Johnson's early career, was dead many years before the " Life " was commenced.

When the time comes for a biography to be written, it is often difficult to obtain details of the hero. Many of his youthful contemporaries are dead, and he himself, having attained distinction and competence, is not always willing to look back on the difficulties of his early days. Mrs. Piozzi relates a story of Johnson bursting into a passion of tears, as he read the lines from his own satire which tell of the "ills which assail the scholar's life," and which were probably founded on his own experience. Boswell, the most diligent of biographers, is obliged to confess that not much could be ascertained about this period of Johnson's life.

On his first arrival in London, he hired a room in Exeter Street, Strand, at the house of Mr. Norris, a stay-maker, and we know something of his manner of living from his own description. "I dined," said he, "very well for eightpence, with very good company, at the 'Pine Apple,' in New Street, just by. Several of them had travelled. They expected to meet every day, but we did not know each other's names. It used to cost the rest a shilling, for they drank wine; but I had a cut of meat for sixpence, and bread for a penny, and gave the waiter a penny, so that I was quite as well served, nay, better, than the rest, for they gave the waiter nothing." He had previously learned, from an Irish painter, whom he had known at Birmingham, the art of "living in a garret on eighteen pence a week," and it was now necessary to turn this knowledge to a practical use. But, notwithstanding economy and self-denial, his finances began to run short, and he was obliged to apply for assistance to Mr. Wilcox, a bookseller in the Strand, who, seeing his burly form, told him he had better buy a porter's knot. The advice was not encouraging, but Wilcox proved to be one of

Johnson's best friends, and not only advanced him money, but also, it appears, found him literary work. After a few months in London, he moved to Greenwich, where he had rooms in Church Street, next door to the Golden Hart, an old tavern that has long since disappeared. From there he wrote to Edward Cave, the editor and proprietor of *The Gentleman's Magazine*, and proposed to translate a French version, which had lately appeared, of Paul Sarpi's "History of the Council of Trent." His offer was accepted, and though nothing appears to have been done in the matter at that time, it brought him into connection with a periodical which for some years afforded his principal means of support.

Edward Cave had been educated at Rugby. He was afterwards employed in the printing office of Alderman John Barber, the friend and correspondent of Swift, and had perhaps helped in printing that writer's celebrated pamphlet, "The Public Spirit of the Whigs," for which Barber and the publisher, Morphew, were summoned to the bar of the House of Lords. When, by diligence and economy, Cave had saved sufficient money, he set up business for himself; and in 1732 commenced *The Gentleman's Magazine*, one of the most useful books of reference in our language, which is still continued, with the old engraving, on the covers, of St. John's Gate, where he resided for many years, and carried on the business of the miscellany. So great was his interest in the enterprise that it was said he "never looked out of the window, but with a view to *The Gentleman's Magazine*," and when he was able to afford a carriage of his own, he had painted on the door panels a view of the ancient building. Here, through his new contributor, Cave made the acquaintance of Garrick, who, long before he appeared on the public stage, got up a representation of Fielding's "Mock Doctor," which was acted in the room over the great arch. The principal character was taken by Garrick, and the other parts read by the journeymen printers.

Hawkins gives an interesting account of the early writers in the magazine. The best known of these was Nicholas Amhurst, who had been expelled from Oxford for some offence, of which his own account differed considerably from that of the college authorities who pronounced the sentence. He had some share in conducting *The Craftsman*, but he was eventually deserted by his patrons, and died of a broken heart in 1742. His funeral expenses were paid by Benjamin Franklin, the printer. Another of the contributors was Samuel Boyse, the poet, who was constantly in distress from his extravagant habits. This strange character could not eat his beef without ketchup sauce, and Johnson said that he would lay out his last half-guinea on truffles and mushrooms, when he was confined to his bed for want of a shirt. He died, in 1749, at an obscure lodging in Shoe Lane. But the chief glory of the magazine was Moses Browne, and Johnson, as a great favour, was taken by Cave to an alehouse at Clerkenwell that he might have the honour of seeing in the flesh this great dignitary of letters, who was found "sitting at the head of a long table in a cloud of tobacco smoke."

At the end of the summer, Johnson made a short trip to Lichfield, but soon returned to London accompanied by his wife, and took rooms—first in Woodstock Street, Hanover Square, and afterwards at Castle Street, in the same neighbourhood. Both of these places still exist. He had finished "Irene," but soon found that it is easier to write a tragedy than to get it acted, and he must have been much mortified when the piece was refused. It required indeed little judgment to discover that it was a play which could never be a favourite with the public. It doubtless shows signs of a vigorous mind, not wanting in imagination, and it would be possible to point out passages of power and dignity which would be admired in the days when Addison's "Cato" was still often given at the theatre, and Blackmore's "Creation" and Glover's "Leonidas" were thought to be noble poems. But, whatever might be the intrinsic merits of the piece, it contained none of those touches of nature which appeal to the sympathy of an audience. The story may be told in a few words. Mahomet the Great, Emperor of the Turks, is fascinated by the charms of Irene, a Greek captive, and asks her to share his throne, but the lady for a time is obdurate, and turns a deaf ear to the prayers of her royal lover. The closing lines of Mahomet's final appeal to Irene are written in direct imitation of Pope, and are not unworthy of their model.

> " If greatness please thee, mount th' imperial seat,
> If pleasure charm thee, view this soft retreat ;
> Here ev'ry warbler of the sky shall sing ;
> Here ev'ry fragrance breathe of ev'ry spring:
> To deck these bow'rs each region shall combine,
> And e'en our prophet's gardens envy thine :
> Empire and Love shall share the blissful day,
> And varied life steal unperceiv'd away."

In the meanwhile a conspiracy, of which Cali, the Grand Vizier, is the chief, is formed against the sovereign, but is detected by the fidelity of two Turkish officers, Hasan and Caraza.   Cali is seized and perishes on the rack, but in his dying moments he falsely denounces Irene as one of the conspirators.   The Greek beauty, who has just consented to become Mahomet's wife, is led away to be strangled, and the Sultan discovers too late he has been deceived.   This story, which can hardly be called a plot, is worked out with little dramatic skill in five long acts, and Mr. Fleetwood, the patentee of Drury Lane, was certainly wise in declining to accept it.

In 1738 Johnson had become one of the regular contributors to *The Gentleman's Magazine*, but his most important work during that year was his "London," written in imitation of the third "Satire of Juvenal," and intended partly as an attack on the Ministry of Walpole.   The poem, as might be expected, shows a want of experience of the world, and many of its sentiments are opposed to those held by Johnson in later days.   The ruin of the nation is attributed to the venality of the Government and the luxury of the great ; the profligate life of the capital is contrasted with the innocent pleasures of the country, and the only hope for England, according to the poet, is to recover her lost liberties, and return to the simple manners of the past. One of the couplets must sometimes have occurred to his hearers, when Johnson was indulging in his sallies against the Scotch, though no one ever probably ventured to quote it, at least in the author's hearing.

" For who would leave, unbrib'd, Hibernia's land,
   Or change the rocks of Scotland for the Strand."

Although much inferior to his later poem, "The Vanity of Human Wishes," it is a fine performance, and immediately attracted attention. Lyttelton took it to Pope, who wished to know the author's name, and declared that he would soon be *déterré.* Johnson received ten guineas for the copyright, and said that he might have accepted less, but that "Paul Whitehead had just received that sum for a poem, and he could not take less than Paul Whitehead."

The poem alluded to was probably "Manners," which, though published later, was written about this time, and its author, a hanger-on of the notorious Bubb Dodington, was chiefly employed in writing satires against the Government, though his pen was pretty much at the service of any one who would pay for his assistance. Johnson had a prejudice against Whitehead, who certainly bore no very favourable reputation, but it does not appear that they were ever acquainted.

At the same time as the publication of Johnson's "London," the first of Pope's two dialogues appeared, under the title of "Seventeen Hundred and Thirty-eight." It was one of his most brilliant and pointed satires, full of personal allusions, introduced with extraordinary skill, and showed the intimate knowledge of passing events which he derived from Bolingbroke. Those who wish to know something of the political history of the time, when Johnson was beginning his literary career, should read the admirable introduction to the dialogues, now known as "The Epilogue to the Satires," in Mr. Courthope's edition of Pope's Works.

From the success of his poem, Johnson derived little

advantage except fame, and he once more turned his thoughts to his old occupation. The mastership of a school, supposed to be that of Appleby, in Leicestershire, was now vacant, but it was necessary that the office should be held by a Master of Arts, and Johnson had not remained long enough at Oxford to obtain a degree. A letter was written by Lord Gower to some friend of Swift, requesting that the Dean's influence might be used with the University of Dublin to procure the necessary diploma. It is not known to whom the letter was written, but in any case the application was unsuccessful, and to this failure has been foolishly attributed Johnson's strong dislike both to Swift and Lord Gower. The latter, indeed, was afterwards for other reasons mentioned, in the dictionary, as an illustration of the word *renegado*, but the printer was wise enough to strike out the name. The following curious note, in Pope's writing, now in the possession of Mr. S. Timmins, F.S.A., of Birmingham, which was sent by the poet to Richardson, with a copy of " London," refers to this incident :—

" This is imitated by one Johnson, who put in for a Publick School in Shropshire, but was Disappointed. He has an Infirmity, of the Convulsive kind, that attacks Him sometimes, so as to make Him a sad spectacle. Mr. P., from the Merits of This work, which was all the knowledge He had of Him, endeavour'd to serve Him without his own Application ; & wrote to my L^d gore, but He did not Succeed. Mr. Johnson publish'd afterw^d another Poem, in Latin, with notes the whole very Humerous, call'd The ' Norfolk Prophecy.'

" P."

Pope seems to have forgotten the Latin translation of his "Messiah," and his description of "The Norfolk Prophecy" shows that he knew little of that work, which had recently been published under the title of "Marmor Norfolciense; or, an Essay on an Ancient Prophetical Inscription in Monkish Rhyme, lately discovered near Lynne in Norfolk, by Probus Britannicus." It is a satire against the Hanoverian dynasty, and relates to the pretended discovery of an ancient stone with engraved characters, near Lynn, which was, of course, chosen as being the nearest town to Houghton Hall, the seat of Sir Robert Walpole. It is not very amusing, and attracted little observation at the time, though it was afterwards reprinted by some political adversary to annoy its author, when he had accepted a pension from the king.

From 1740 to 1743, Johnson was actively employed in preparing the reports of the parliamentary debates for *The Gentleman's Magazine.* At first he merely revised the version prepared by Guthrie, a Scotchman of great learning, then in Cave's employ, but afterwards he had to draw up the speeches from the notes of the reporters, who, by Cave's interest with the doorkeepers, managed to get access to the House; and occasionally he was only supplied with the names of those who had taken part in the debate. These speeches, owing to the strict regulations against publishing anything which took place in Parliament, appeared as "Debates in Magna Lilliputia," and fictitious names were assigned to the speakers. The reports, which showed a thorough knowledge of the subjects under discussion, and of the style and peculiarities of the leading statesmen, were generally accepted as genuine, and their real authorship was not discovered till some years later.

Mr. Murphy relates that at a dinner party at Mr. Foote's, an important debate, towards the end of Sir Robert Walpole's Administration, being mentioned, Dr. Francis observed "that Mr. Pitt's speech on that occasion was the best he had ever read." He went on to say that "he had employed eight years of his life in the study of Demosthenes, and finished a translation of that celebrated orator, with all the decorations of style and language within the reach of his capacity; but he had met with nothing equal to the speech above mentioned." Many of the company remembered the debate; and some passages were cited with the approbation and applause of all present. During the ardour of conversation, Johnson remained silent. As soon as the warmth of praise subsided, he opened with these words: "That speech I wrote in a garret in Exeter Street." The guests then began to praise the impartiality with which reason and eloquence had been equally dealt out to both parties. But Johnson would not agree to this. "I saved," he said, "appearances tolerably well, but I took care that the *Whig dogs* should not have the best of it."

Besides the parliamentary reports, he wrote at this time several short biographies and other contributions to the magazine, and he had also a large share in preparing the catalogue of Lord Oxford's library, recently purchased by Osborne, a well-known bookseller, who had the misfortune to occupy, in the later editions of "The Dunciad," the place originally given to Chapman in the ignoble contest with Curll. While engaged in this work, Johnson had an unfortunate controversy with his employer, which ended in his knocking down the bookseller with one of the folio volumes of the collection. The details of the quarrel are not accurately known, and when questioned by Mrs. Thrale on the subject, he said: "There is nothing to tell, dearest lady, but that he was insolent, and I beat him; and that he was a block-head, and told of it. I have beat many a fellow, but the rest had the wit to hold their tongues."

In addition to his literary work, Johnson was now a good deal engaged with the business affairs of his old friend, Thomas Warren, the bookseller, who had entered into partnership with John Wyatt and Lewis Paul. These gentlemen had established a cotton mill at Birmingham, where the first essay was made at spinning by rollers. Some of the letters, referring to this transaction, are given in Croker's edition of the "Life," but the interesting correspondence, relating to this subject, was destroyed, when the Free Library at Birmingham was burnt down in 1879.

The Gentleman's Magazine had now established a high position, and numbered among its contributors Savage, Birch, Hawkesworth, and Miss Elizabeth Carter, who were all afterwards well known in the literary world. With these colleagues Johnson was more or less intimate, and his old Lichfield acquaintance, Henry Hervey, who had married Molly Aston's sister, had now a house in London, where Johnson was often a visitor. To the last day of his life he was never tired of alluding to the kindness received from this friend of his early days, and only a short time before his death he said : "If you call a dog Hervey, I shall love him."

In the summer of 1743 Richard Savage, a friend of a very different stamp from the polished Hervey, died in Bristol, where he had been for some time detained in prison for debt. Johnson undertook to write his life, and announced his intention in a letter to *The Gentleman's Magazine.* Savage had left London in July, 1739, and had promised to settle quietly in Wales, on the understanding that he should receive a yearly allowance of £50, of which nearly half was contributed by Pope, to whom Savage had been useful in supplying information for "The Dunciad," about the private lives of the Grub Street authors. It would be difficult to find, even in fiction, any career more strange than that of this extraordinary character. He asserted that he was the son of Lord Rivers, and that his mother was the Countess of Macclesfield, who, from the time of his birth, had never lost an opportunity of doing him every injury in her power. She had, he alleged, prevented his father, on his death-bed, from making any provision for his son, by falsely stating that he was no longer living ; she had constantly refused either to see him or to help him ; and she had even endeavoured to defeat the attempts of his friends to procure the royal clemency, when he lay under sentence of death for killing a man in a pothouse brawl. Judge Page, of whom Pope, in allusion to this event, wrote,

"Hard words or hanging if your judge be Page,"

[1] "Satire," i. 82.

presided at the trial, and he afterwards confessed that he had treated the prisoner with great harshness. A brief "Life of Savage," sometimes attributed to Defoe, with all the particulars of the unfortunate man's history, appeared shortly after the trial, and no doubt helped to influence public opinion in his favour. A pardon was at length granted, and after his release he gratified his feelings of revenge towards his unnatural mother by publishing "The Bastard; a Poem, incribed with all due reverence to Mrs. Bret, once Countess of Macclesfield. By Richard Savage, son of the late Earl Rivers."

It will probably never be known what foundation Savage had for his strange story. It was, at all events, believed by men like Steele and Johnson; and Lord Tyrconnel, himself a nephew of Lady Macclesfield, was one of Savage's kindest patrons, till he was disgusted with his *protégé's* brutality. This profligate woman, who survived till 1753, is stated by Boswell to have been of some assistance to Colley Cibber in his play of "The Careless Husband," and to have suggested to him the idea of one of its best scenes from an incident in her own life. Her eldest daughter by her second husband, Colonel Brett, was for a short time the mistress of George I., and, after the death of that sovereign, became the wife of Sir William Leman. In the announcement of the marriage which appeared in *The Gentleman's Magazine*, she is described as "Miss Bret, half-sister to Mr. Savage, son to the late Earl Rivers."

When Johnson first made acquaintance with Savage it is, as stated in the previous chapter, impossible to ascertain. Boswell declares it was not till after May, 1738, but in that case, as Savage was never in London after July, 1739, their personal intercourse would have lasted little more than a year, which is scarcely consistent with the intimacy known to have existed between them.

Johnson's "Life of Savage" appeared in 1744. Boswell states that it was composed with great rapidity, and that forty-eight printed octavo pages were written at one sitting; but there could have been no valid reason for this haste, as the work was not published for six months after it had been announced. Though occasionally rather overlarded with moral sentiments, and not sufficiently precise in details, it is a delightful piece of biography, full of graphic descriptions and curious facts, many of which the writer must have related from personal knowledge. Reynolds was told by Johnson that one night, "when Savage and he walked round St. James's Square, for want of a lodging, they were not at all depressed by their situation; but, in high spirits and brimful of patriotism, traversed the square for several hours, inveighed against the Ministry, and resolved they would *stand by their country*." Johnson had a strange partiality for Savage, whose claims to literary distinction were slight, and whose private life was disgraced by falsehood, rapacity, and ingratitude.

"The Life of Savage" was much admired, but its author was still miserably poor; and his appearance was so shabby that he was ashamed to be seen in public. A story is told of his dinner being sent to him behind a screen on an occasion when some friend was dining with Cave; but the conversation happened to turn on the new book, and Johnson had the pleasure of hearing his work highly commended.

For the next two years he appears to have assisted in editing *The Gentleman's Magazine,* and little is known to have been written by him, except the "Miscellaneous Observations on Macbeth," which were praised by Warburton, "at a time," as he said, "when praise was of value."

About this time he entered into an agreement with a syndicate of booksellers to compile an English Dictionary for the sum of fifteen hundred and seventy-five pounds, and the undertaking was announced to the public, in 1747, by his "Plan of a Dictionary of the English Language," addressed to the Earl of Chesterfield. Nothing could be more clear or scholarlike than the principles which he had laid down for carrying out his scheme, and he frequently illustrated his meaning, and showed the necessity of such a work, by passages from the best-known authors. But some years elapsed before the Dictionary appeared, of which there will be more to say hereafter.

In 1748 a visit was paid to Tunbridge Wells, and in a contemporary drawing, afterwards engraved for Mrs. Barbauld's "Life of Richardson," there are portraits of Johnson and his wife. She had been latterly in declining health, and a part of the summer was passed by them at Hampstead, where he wrote "The Vanity of Human Wishes," an imitation of the third "Satire of Juvenal," and it appeared early in the ensuing year. This poem has never been sufficiently known or appreciated. When first published, it was thought inferior to his "London," and Garrick pronounced it to be hard as Greek. It certainly lacks the sweetness of Goldsmith, and it never attains the polished versification of Pope, but in its own manner it is unsurpassed. The tendency of the satire is perhaps mournful, but scarcely more so than the treatment which the subject requires. Every phase of "motley life" is passed in review, and the different careers of the churchman, the politician, the soldier, and the statesman are touched upon with great beauty and force. In each case the moral is the same, "The Vanity of Human Wishes." The description of the placid old age which rewards an innocent and a temperate life has an especial interest.

> " An age that melts with unperceiv'd decay,
> And glides in modest innocence away ;
> Whose peaceful day Benevolence endears,
> Whose night congratulating Conscience cheers ;
> The gen'ral fav'rite as the gen'ral friend :
> Such age there is, and who shall wish its end?"

These touching lines refer to the poet's mother, who was then in her eightieth year. Those who are familiar with the literature of that period will easily recognize how much this poem must have influenced Goldsmith in his "Traveller" and "Deserted Village," though in tenderness and simplicity he undoubtedly far surpassed his model.

CHAPTER IV

A N important event was now to occur in Johnson's life. His tragedy of "Irene" was at length to be produced on the stage by Garrick, who was then manager of Drury Lane Theatre. Some alterations were however necessary to render the play more suited for the stage, and these the author was very unwilling to allow, but Garrick insisted on their being carried out. "Sir," said Johnson, "the fellow wants me to make Mahomet run mad, that he may have an opportunity of tossing his hands and kicking his heels." But the difficulty was at length overcome through the intervention of their common friend, Dr. Taylor, and the piece was acted on Monday, February 6, 1749, under the title of "Mahomet and Irene." Everything had been done by the manager to obtain success; new decorations and costumes were supplied; Garrick played Demetrius and gave up the part of Mahomet to Mr. Barry, to ensure the more hearty co-operation of that celebrated actor; Mrs. Pritchard took the part of the heroine, and Aspasia was played by Mrs. Cibber, whose musical voice and classic beauty gave her great advantages in tragedy. The epilogue, which is bright and humorous, was said to be from the pen of Sir William Yonge, the "Sir Billy," of Pope's Satires, and was well adapted to send away the audience in good humour. Johnson was present at every performance in a scarlet waistcoat, trimmed with gold lace, and a laced hat, which he soon afterwards discarded, as he pretended " that, when in that dress, he could not treat people with the same ease as when in his usual plain clothes."

There are several accounts extant by those who were present on the first night, but that which Dr. Adams gave Boswell is perhaps the most trustworthy. " Before the curtain drew up there were catcalls whistling which alarmed Johnson's friends. The prologue, which was written by himself in a manly strain, soothed the audience, and the play went off tolerably till it came to the conclusion, when Mrs. Pritchard, the heroine of the piece, was to be strangled on the stage, and was to speak two lines with the bow-string round her neck. The audience cried out "Murder! Murder!" She several times attempted to speak, but in vain. At last she was obliged to go off the stage alive." The author's annoyance at this interruption must have been a good deal alleviated by the triumph it gave him over Garrick, at whose suggestion the strangling scene had been arranged.

Dr. Burney's version is more favourable, but he speaks of a curious story circulated at the time of the author's being "observed at the representation to be dissatisfied with some of the speeches and conduct of the play himself, and, like La Fontaine, expressing his disapprobation aloud."

Old Aaron Hill, one of the heroes of "The Dunciad,"

who had composed much bad poetry and worse prose, and whose critical judgment may be estimated by his prediction of his own posthumous fame and of Pope's speedy oblivion, wrote to Mallet: "I was at the anomalous Mr. Johnson's benefit, and found the play his proper representative ; strong sense, ungraced by sweetness or decorum." Though Irene was not a great success, it escaped positive failure, and Johnson received from copyright and "author's nights," very nearly three hundred pounds.

The year after the performance of "Irene," the first number of *The Rambler* was published, on the 20th March, 1750, and the periodical, which appeared every Tuesday and Saturday, was continued without interruption for two years. With the exception of four or five numbers, it was entirely written by Johnson, and shows remarkable fertility of mind when it is remembered that during that time he was also occupied with his Dictionary besides other literary work. *The Rambler* must be confessed to come under Charles Lamb's unflattering definition, as one of those books which no gentleman's library should be without, and, we fear, it might be added, that its volumes are seldom taken down from the shelves. The wits of the day pretended that the author had used hard words to make his forthcoming dictionary indispensable, and Burke said that the ladies in *The Rambler* were all "Johnsons in petticoats." This is, of course, exaggeration. The work has, perhaps, too many abstract discussions on moral and religious subjects to please the general reader, and there are no traces of the refined humour of Addison, or of the strange pathos of Steele, but a pleasant hour may often be passed in looking through its numbers, and some are not without interest. The papers, which contain letters from fictitious correspondents, are clearly imitated from those in *The Tatler* and *Spectator*; but the essayists of the time of Queen Anne were chiefly men of the world and their writings show an experience of life and society which a scholar of limited means, with a sick wife, could scarcely be expected to possess. One of the chief defects of *The Rambler* is that little is to be learnt in it of the social life of the epoch, though some of the characters show a considerable knowledge of human nature, and from the sketch of Suspirius in the 59th number, Goldsmith confessed that he had borrowed his idea of Mr. Crook in "The Good-natured Man."

Shortly after the appearance of the last number of *The Rambler*, Mrs. Johnson died, on the 28th March, 1752, and, though at last her life was said to be nothing but "perpetual illness and perpetual opium," her loss was deeply felt by her husband. Many years after, when his old fellow collegian, Edwards, asked him if he had ever known what it was to have a wife, Johnson replied, with a faltering voice: "Sir, I have known what it was to have a wife, and I have known what it was to *lose a wife*. It had almost broke my heart." He had many kind friends to console him in his bereavement, and soon after his wife's death, Mrs. Williams became an inmate of his house; but his real solace was probably in the work of his dictionary, which now seems to have engrossed the chief share of his attention.

It is necessary to say a few words about Mrs. Williams,

whose name is so familiar to all readers of Boswell's
"Life." This interesting person was the daughter of a
Welsh physician, who had some pretensions to be a man
of science, and laboured under a delusion that he had
discovered the means of ascertaining the longitude. She
herself had dabbled in poetry, but was blind before she
knew Johnson, and an operation for cataract, which she
underwent in his house, had been unsuccessful. Miss
Hawkins describes her as "a pale shrunken old lady,
dressed in scarlet, made in the handsome French fashion
of the time, with a lace cap, with two stiffened projecting
wings on the temples and a black lace hood over it."
Her temper was not always under control, but her
genuine worth, and excellent common sense, made her
a favourite with many of Johnson's friends, and Boswell
records with great pride the first occasion, when he was
taken home to drink tea with Mrs. Williams. There is
an engraved portrait of her from a miniature by Miss
Reynolds.

We have a glimpse of Johnson in a letter, written in
July of this year, by Mrs. Chapone to Miss Elizabeth
Carter, then one of the regular contributors to *The
Gentleman's Magazine*: "We had a visit, whilst at
Northend, from your friend, Mr. Johnson, and poor
Mrs. Williams. I was charmed with his behaviour to
her, which was like that of a fond father to his daughter.
She seemed much pleased with her visit; showed very
good sense, with a great deal of modesty and humility,
and so much patience and cheerfulness under her mis-
fortune, that it doubled my concern for her. Mr.
Johnson was very communicative and entertaining, and

did me the honour to address most of his discourse
to me."

The Grange, North End, Fulham, where Richardson
lived, is still (1887) in existence, though the part of the
house, which he occupied, has since been covered with
white stucco, but, in the other half, the red brick walls are
unchanged. There is an engraving of the picturesque
old building in vol. iv. of " Richardson's Correspondence," 1804.

The Dictionary was still progressing. In 1753 the second
volume was begun, and in the following year the laborious
task was at length finished to the great joy, no less of
the compiler than of the publishers, whose patience
was nearly worn out by constant delays in the work.
" Thank God I have done with him ! " exclaimed Mr.
Millar, who had charge of the publication, when he
received the last sheets. "I am glad," said Johnson,
when he heard of the bookseller's expression, " that he
thanks God for anything." He always, however, spoke
kindly of Millar, who, he said, " had raised the price of
literature."

In the summer of 1754, Johnson paid a visit to Oxford,
which he had not seen since he left it as an undergraduate.
His old tutor, Mr. Jorden, was dead, and Dr. Adams
does not seem to have been in residence ; but he had a
cordial meeting with his former rival, Meeke, who had
now become a Fellow, and he was delighted to find himself remembered by the college servants.

Early in 1755 the degree of M.A. was conferred upon
him by the University, and he was no doubt especially
pleased that the diploma was placed in his hands by Dr.

William King, Principal of St. Mary's Hall, a wit and a scholar, and a strong adherent of the old dynasty. Some years later, when this "idol of the Jacobites" had to take part at the installation of the Earl of Westmoreland as Chancellor of the University, Johnson, who had been present at the ceremony, wrote—" I have clapped my hands, till they are sore, at Dr. King's speech."

On April 15th, the Dictionary was issued to the public in two folio volumes, price, bound £4 4s. It had a great success, went rapidly through several editions, and in some form or another is to this day constantly being re-printed. Its weak point is said to be in the derivations, but the study of philology had in those days received little attention, and to judge from the disputes among its modern professors it is still anything but an exact science. Some of the definitions caused much amuse-ment, and certainly that, so often quoted, of *Network*— "anything reticulated or decussated at equal distances with interstices between the intersections,"—throws little light on the subject. In some cases the lexicographer took the opportunity of displaying his personal feelings. *Oats* is defined as "a grain which in England is given to horses, but in Scotland supports the people." Sir Walter Scott tells of the happy retort by Lord Elibank, who, when he heard of Johnson's definition of "Oats," said : " Yes ; and where else will you see *such* horses and *such* men ? "

The illustrations of the various meanings and uses of words is the most valuable part of the work, and shows an extraordinary knowledge of literature. Johnson's method of compilation was very simple. He began by reading the works of those authors whom he thought to be trustworthy authorities, and underlined with a pencil, not the sentence, as both Dr. Percy and Boswell assert, but the word[1] which he intended to use, and wrote the initial letters on the margin, with vertical lines before and after the passage. The sentences, where these pencil marks occurred, were copied by his clerks on separate slips, and pasted into an interleaved copy of some old dictionary, opposite the words they were to illustrate.

The " Plan for a Dictionary," published in 1747, had been, as before mentioned, dedicated to Lord Chesterfield, who was now anxious that his name should appear as the patron of the Dictionary itself. But Johnson was very indignant at the neglect with which he had been treated, and was not at all conciliated by two very flattering papers, written by Lord Chesterfield in *The World*. "He had," said Johnson, "for many years taken no notice of me, but when my Dictionary was coming out, he fell a-scribbling in *The World* about it. Upon which I wrote him a letter, expressed in civil terms, but such as might show him that I did not mind what he said and wrote, and that I had done with him." The letter which he sent on that occasion is, though short, one of the finest productions of his pen. Its manly tone, its rugged pathos, the dignity of its style, and the cold severity of the invective, can never be surpassed.

[1] So it appears at least to have been done in Johnson's copy of Drayton's " Polyolbion," now in the possession of Mr. Samuel Timmins, F.S.A., of Birmingham.

"To the Earl of Chesterfield.

"*February* 7, 1755.

"My Lord,—I have been lately informed by the proprietor of *The World*, that two papers, in which my Dictionary is recommended to the public, were written by your lordship. To be so distinguished is an honour, which, being very little accustomed to favours from the great, I know not well how to receive, or in what terms to acknowledge.

"When, upon some slight encouragement, I first visited your lordship, I was overpowered, like the rest of mankind, by the enchantment of your address, and could not forbear to wish that I might boast myself *Le vainqueur du vainqueur de la terre;*—that I might obtain that regard for which I saw the world contending; but I found my attendance so little encouraged, that neither pride nor modesty would suffer me to continue it. When I had once addressed your lordship in public, I had exhausted all the art of pleasing which a retired and uncourtly scholar can possess. I had done all that I could; and no man is well pleased to have his all neglected, be it ever so little.

"Seven years, my lord, have now passed, since I waited in your outward rooms, or was repulsed from your door; during which time I have been pushing on my work through difficulties, of which it is useless to complain, and have brought it, at last, to the verge of publication, without one act of assistance, one word of encouragement, or one smile of favour. Such treatment I did not expect, for I never had a patron before.

"The shepherd in Virgil grew at last acquainted with Love, and found him a native of the rocks.

"Is not a patron, my lord, one who looks with unconcern on a man struggling for life in the water, and when he has reached ground, encumbers him with help? The notice which you have been pleased to take of my labours, had it been early, had been kind; but it has been delayed till I am indifferent, and cannot enjoy it; till I am solitary, and cannot impart it; till I am known, and do not want it. I hope it is no very cynical asperity not to confess obligations where no benefit has been received, or to be unwilling that the public should consider me as owing that to a patron, which Providence has enabled me to do for myself.

"Having carried on my work thus far with so little obligation to any favourer of learning, I shall not be disappointed though I should conclude, if less be possible, with less; for I have been long wakened from that dream of hope, in which I once boasted myself with so much exultation. My Lord, your lordship's most humble, most obedient servant,

"SAM. JOHNSON."

Lord Chesterfield showed uncommon wisdom in not attempting a reply, but he made some efforts to appease Johnson through the mediation of Sir Thomas Robinson, who had been one of the puppets in the Duke of Newcastle's Ministry. It was an unlucky choice. Sir Thomas, one of the most notorious bores in London, used to pester his chief with visits, and when told his grace was engaged, he would ask permission to look at the clock, or play with the monkey in the hall. At last even the lacqueys lost patience, and one day, when Sir Thomas called, the porter, without giving him time to speak, said, "Sir, his grace is out, the clock has stopped, and the monkey is dead." His interview with Johnson was short and unsuccessful, and the Yorkshire baronet seems to have narrowly escaped being shown out of the room.

In this year he renewed his correspondence with his schoolfellow, Hector, to whom he wrote: "I was extremely pleased to find you have not forgotten your old friend, who yet recollects the evenings which we have passed together at Warren's. . . . Since we have again renewed our acquaintance, do not let us intermit it so long again. . . . What news of poor Warren? I have not lost all my kindness for him, for when I remember you, I naturally remember all our connexions, which are more pleasing to me for your sake."

Johnson's financial affairs had not been improved by the success of his Dictionary; twice in the year after its publication, he had to appeal to Richardson for help, and, on one of these occasions, the kindness of the novelist was required to release him from arrest. He seems to have written little for some time after the completion of his great work. The death of his friend, Cave, in 1754, had probably severed his close connection with *The Gentleman's Magazine*, and he was a good deal occupied with the affairs of Mr. Paul, one of the owners of the cotton mill at Birmingham.

In 1758, he began a new series of essays, under the name of "The Idler," the first of which appeared on April 15th, in the second number of *The Universal Chronicle.*

It is lighter reading, and more amusing than *The Rambler*, though it never attained the same reputation as its predecessor.   One or two of the imaginary personages are easily identified.   Jack Whirler is taken from John Newbery, the bookseller, and the writer himself is depicted under the name of Sober.   The character of Dick Minim, who acquired the reputation of a critic, by constantly repeating the commonplace truisms of literature, is drawn with great humour, and was probably taken from life, but the original is not known.   The descriptions of social life are chiefly taken from the lower classes, and are interesting from their circumstantial air of truth.

The forty-first number has a very mournful reality.   It describes the death of the writer's mother, who had attained her ninetieth year.   Johnson was not able to leave London at the time, but his letters show the intensity of his sorrow, and it was no doubt an aggravation of his grief that he could not be present at his mother's last moments, though she was tenderly nursed by Lucy Porter and the faithful old servant Catherine.   The death of his mother severed a great link in his life, and he felt acutely the loneliness of his position.   He writes to his step-daughter that she is the only person left in the world with whom he thinks himself connected, and again, "I have nobody but you."

Soon after this sad event, he composed "Rasselas," to pay for his mother's funeral expenses.   This little Eastern story, the most pleasing and the best known of his writings, was published on April 19, 1759, sixteen days after the appearance of Goldsmith's "Enquiry into the Present State of Polite Learning."   It has been remarked as a curious coincidence that Voltaire's "Candide," and " Rasselas," appeared about the same time, but far too much importance has been given by critics to the fancied resemblance between the two works. "Candide," which is ostensibly written in ridicule of optimism, is a very thinly disguised attack on religion, and holds up to bitter scorn the best feelings of our nature. A husband's regard for his wife's honour, the ties of family, the duties of friendship, the tender feelings of love, are all treated with contempt and irony. It is Voltaire's most powerful satire, but the resemblance, which it bears to "Rasselas," is very superficial.

Johnson's object was neither to ridicule nor to complain of the decrees of fate, but to show that no condition of life can be entirely free from misfortune ; and the endeavours of the Eastern despot, in the story, to banish care and sorrow from the happy valley are proved to be impossible. It is difficult to refrain from quoting from this work a passage of exceeding beauty, which contains one of the most touching and poetic similes in the language. It occurs in Imlac's conversation with the princess, when he is endeavouring to console her for the loss of her beloved friend, the Lady Pekuah: "The state of a mind, oppressed with a sudden calamity," said Imlac, "is like that of the fabulous inhabitants of the new created earth, who, when the first night came upon them, supposed that day would never return. When the clouds of sorrow gather over us, we see nothing beyond them, nor can imagine how they will be dispelled ; yet a new day succeeded to the night, and sorrow is never long without a dawn of ease."

A curious tribute of praise is given to "Rasselas" in

Dr. Oliver Wendell Holmes's recent novel, "A Mortal Antipathy." In a lecture on Delusions, supposed to be delivered by Dr. Butts, one of the characters of the story, he says, " But if you ask me what reading I would recommend to the medical student of a philosophical habit of mind, you may be surprised to hear me say it would be certain passages in 'Rasselas.' They are the ones where the astronomer gives an account to Imlac of his management of the elements, the control of which, as he had persuaded himself, had been committed to him."

It may be interesting to the reader to know something of the places, a few of which have been already alluded to, where Johnson was living during the early part of his London life. In 1748, he took a house in Gough Square, where his wife died in 1752, and here he wrote The Dictionary, *The Rambler*, the greater part of *The Idler*, and " Rasselas." Soon after the completion of this last work in 1759, he hired rooms in Staple Inn, and on the 23rd of March he wrote to Lucy Porter that his things were that day moved to his new abode. In December, of the same year, we learn, from the heading of a letter to Mrs. Montagu, that he was living in Gray's Inn, which he left sometime, in 1761, for chambers on the first floor of No. 1, Inner Temple Lane, and he remained there till 1766, when he took a house in Johnson's Court.

We learn something of Johnson's friends and manner of life in 1761, and 1762, from two delightful letters which he wrote to Baretti, who was then staying at Milan. They are too long to quote in full, but a summary will give an idea of their contents. The first piece of news is that Fitzherbert was elected a member of the new Parliament. This gentleman had married Miss Meynell, one of Johnson's early friends, whom he had met in former days when stopping at Ashbourne. He had a great admiration for her beauty and virtues, and declared she had the best understanding of any human being he had ever met. A few lines further on we read that the artists had just closed their second exhibition of pictures and statues. This was held in an auctioneer's room at Spring Gardens, and the catalogue contained a frontispiece and tailpiece by Hogarth. There was, however, a rival exhibition in the room of the Society of Arts, and it may have been that to which the letter alludes. He goes oftener, he writes, to the theatre, where many new farces have been produced, and he has lately seen Colman's last comedy of "The Jealous Wife." In this piece one of the characters was taken by Mrs. Clive, who, Johnson always said, was the best player he ever saw.

. In the second letter of July 20, 1762, he tells Baretti that he had sent him a copy of *The Idler* and he was soon to send a copy of his edition of Shakespeare, whose works Baretti might explain to the Italian ladies, and tell them "the story of the editor, among other strange narratives with which your long residence in this unknown region has supplied you." He and Mrs. Williams were living "much as they did." Mrs. Porter, the actress, was still with Miss Cotterel, and Charlotte was now expecting her fourth child.[1] Reynolds was making £6,000 a year. Levett was lately married, not without

[1] The two latter ladies were daughters of Admiral Cotterel, who used to live opposite Johnson in Castle Street, Cavendish Square. Charlotte was then the wife of the Rev. John Lewis.

much suspicion that he has been wretchedly cheated in the match.[1] Richardson, the author, had died of an apoplexy, and his daughter was married to a merchant. The next item of news is personal. The writer had been, the previous winter, at Lichfield, and found that his playfellows had grown old, and he himself was no longer young. Lucy Porter (whom, by a strange error, for the author of a dictionary, he calls daughter-in-law) had lost the beauty and gaiety of youth, but he had "met her with sincere benevolence." It was probably a quarter of a century since they had seen one another, and during that time Lucy Porter, now forty-six years of age, had no doubt considerably changed. After five days at his native town, he had seized the first opportunity of returning to London, where he writes, "if there is not much happiness, there is at least such a diversity of good and evil, that slight vexations do not fix upon the heart." The letter ends with a request that Baretti should show all the civilities in his power to Topham Beauclerk, who had always been very kind to the writer, and was then in Italy.

But a great change was to take place in Johnson's life. Since the completion of the Dictionary, his literary labours seem to have consisted chiefly of prefaces and dedications, for the works of friends, and unimportant articles for the magazines. The time, however, was now come when such work would no longer be necessary. He was no more to be harassed by printers waiting for copy,

---

[1] This suspicion soon became a certainty, and both parties seem to have been disappointed. A separation was, however, arranged, and Levett became an inmate of Johnson's house.

or by hearing that publishers had thanked goodness that they had done with him. He had long ago earned fame, and its pleasant accompaniment of competence was now to follow. At the time he was writing to Baretti, he had already accepted a pension from the king, of £300 a year; and, when calling on Lord Bute to thank him for this mark of royal favour, the minister had expressly said to him, " It is not given to you for what you are to do, but for what you have done."

Such an income to a man of Johnson's temperate habits not only enabled him to live in comfort, but it gave him a feeling of independence, which, to a person of his proud and indolent disposition, must have added a new zest to life. He gained something, moreover, which he would value still more; he was now in a position to relieve those cases of want and misery, which never failed to excite his compassion, and how numerous those cases were, not even his most intimate friends ever knew. But his prosperity effected other changes in his life. He was able to mix more freely in that social life, in which he took such a keen delight. The poor author, whose shabby dress obliged him to take his meals behind a screen, when friends were dining with his employer, was to be a guest at the tables of the most distinguished men of the kingdom. The drudge who was " kept waiting in the outer rooms," or " repulsed from the door " of his patron, was, without solicitation, to be honoured by a private interview with his sovereign. He was to become the object of an enthusiastic hero-worship to many, and especially to a young Scotchman, who was, one day, to write a biography of his " illustrious friend," which was to be read wherever the English language is spoken. The famous "Club," which numbered among its members men like Fox and Burke, Goldsmith and Reynolds, was afterwards to be inseparably associated with his name, and he was soon to gather round him that brilliant circle of friends, who are immortalized in the pages of Boswell.

CHAPTER V

THE pension, which had been conferred upon Johnson, added, without doubt, enormously to his happiness, but he must occasionally have felt certain misgivings on the subject. For the political opinions, which he might formerly have expressed, there was no occasion to trouble himself. The Minister, who advised the grant, had not asked him to change his principles, or to give any promises of future support. He would naturally be more guarded in the expression of any partizan feelings, but to this he was quite reconciled. "It is true," he said, "I cannot now curse the House of Hanover, nor would it be decent for me to drink King James's health in the wine, that King George gives me the money to pay for. But, sir, I think that the pleasure of cursing the House of Hanover, and drinking King James's health, are amply compensated for by three hundred pounds a year." The pension was not political; it was especially stated to have been conferred for services rendered to literature. But Johnson had in his dictionary defined *pension* as "an allowance made to any one without an equivalent. In England it is generally understood to mean pay given to a State hireling for treason to his country." No distinction is here drawn between political pensions and those granted for more honourable services, and his adversaries were not slow to take advantage of this omission.

Johnson, moreover, could have had little sympathy with Lord Bute, who was the ostensible mover in the affair. This nobleman, with scant experience of public life, and with no claims to office except his intimacy with the king's mother, had obtained a seat in the Cabinet shortly after the commencement of the new reign, and Pitt, who found his advice no longer heeded, gave up his place as Secretary of State. The Duke of Newcastle, the nominal head of the Government, was delighted to get rid of his brilliant colleague, but soon found that he was not more powerful than before. He still, however, clung to office, but the situation at length became intolerable, and he was forced to resign. Bute immediately became First Lord of the Treasury and Prime Minister.

Johnson was in principle a strong Tory, and his worst term of abuse was to call his adversary a vile Whig, but this seems to have been merely an abstract idea. Nearly all his personal friends belonged to the party for which, in theory, he professed such a strong aversion. He appears, in fact, to have taken little interest in practical politics. During the last years of the reign of George II., the country had been passing through a period of glory such as never was before known in our history. Our armies and navies had been victorious both in the New and Old World, but of these brilliant events, we find no mention in Johnson's recorded conversation, or correspondence ; and politics are never alluded to. In his two long letters to Baretti, referred to in the last chapter, nothing is said of the struggles going on, first between Bute and Pitt, and afterwards between Bute and the Duke of Newcastle. Of mere party feelings, as they are now understood, we could scarcely expect to hear much, for the distinctive lines, which, before and since, have separated the Whigs from the Tories, had then almost entirely disappeared. "The great parties," writes Burke, a few years afterwards, "which formerly divided and agitated the kingdom, are known to be in a manner entirely dissolved." Those, who were willing to comply with the wishes of the sovereign, were called the ' king's friends'; all the rest were branded as factious. George III. hated the elder Pitt as cordially as, in after days, he detested Charles James Fox. "Here is a man," said Johnson, the year before he died, speaking of the latter statesman, "who has divided the kingdom with Cæsar;" but he afterwards declared, that though he was for the king against Fox, he was for Fox against Pitt. Nonentities, like Lord Bute, or the Duke of Newcastle, and men of ability, like Lord North, were equally willing to carry on the Government as mere private secretaries of the king, and to issue orders and to sign decrees for measures, which they knew to be fraught with evil to the country. Johnson's political pamphlets will be alluded to in due course, but they were only episodes in his literary career, and afford little interest or information. It is time, however, to return to the ordinary events of his life.

In 1763, an incident occurred which gave him great satisfaction. Lucy Porter, who, since the death of his mother, was still living with the faithful servant, Kitty, at

Lichfield, and occupied a portion of the old house in the market-place, inherited a fortune of £10,000 from her brother. It had been Johnson's intention that Lucy Porter should live with him in London, as soon as he was able to offer her a comfortable home ; but she was now independent, and resolved to settle at Lichfield. The first use that she made of her new wealth was, much against Johnson's advice, to build a house, which swallowed up nearly a third of her legacy. This spacious and comfortable residence, on Green Hill, is still (1887) almost unchanged, and here Johnson always found a room during his subsequent visits to his native city.

It was in this year that Johnson was introduced to his future biographer. A few years before, when travelling in a post-chaise with Sir David Dalrymple, the object of his first hero-worship, Boswell had heard some anecdotes about Johnson which had inspired him with the ambition of making his acquaintance. Derrick, who, in 1761, had succeeded Beau Nash as "*King of Bath*," had promised to introduce Boswell, during the latter's first visit to London, in 1760, but no opportunity occurred. Thomas Sheridan, the son of Swift's old friend, was lecturing at Edinburgh in the summer of 1761, and had still further excited Boswell's curiosity by many stories of Johnson's eccentricities and wit; but Sheridan and Johnson were now no longer on good terms. The acquaintance was at length made through Mr. Thomas Davies, the bookseller, formerly an actor, who afterwards became an author, and wrote a "Life of Garrick." Boswell's account of his first interview with Johnson is one of the capital passages in his famous "Life." On

Monday, the 16th of May, 1763, Boswell had just finished
drinking tea with Davies and his pretty wife,[1] when the
bookseller saw Johnson through the glass door of the
back parlour where they were sitting, and "announced
his awful approach somewhat in the manner of an actor
in the part of Horatio, when he addresses Hamlet on the
appearance of his father's ghost: 'Look, my Lord, he
comes.' . . . Mr. Davies mentioned my name, and
respectfully introduced me to him. I was much agitated,
and recollecting his prejudice against the Scotch, of
which I had heard much, I said to Davies, 'Don't tell
where I come from.' 'From Scotland,' cried Davies,
roguishly. 'Mr. Johnson,' said I, 'I do indeed come
from Scotland, but I cannot help it.' *Johnson.* That,
sir, I find is what a very great many of your countrymen
cannot help." This was not very encouraging, but the
future biographer soon laid himself open to a more angry
retort. "He (Johnson) then addressed himself to
Davies: 'What do you think of Garrick? He has
refused me an order for the play for Miss Williams,
because he knows the house will be full, and that an
order would be worth three shillings!' Eager to take
any opening to get into conversation with him, I ventured
to say: 'O, sir, I cannot think Mr. Garrick would
grudge such a trifle to you.' 'Sir,' said he, with a stern
look, 'I have known David Garrick longer than you have
done, and I know no right you have to talk to me on
the subject.'" Boswell confessed that the check was
deserved, and thought he had lost all chance of obtain-

[1] "—— upon my life,
That Davies has a pretty wife."—*Churchill.*

ing the intimacy so long the object of his ambition, but he was wise enough to remain quiet, and take no further part in the conversation beyond a few occasional remarks. On his leaving the house, Davies followed him to the door, and tried to comfort him by saying: " Don't be uneasy ; I can see he likes you very well."

Some days after this not very hopeful introduction, Boswell called on Johnson in his chambers, and was well received.   In the course of a few weeks another visit was paid to Inner Temple Lane, and this was followed by an accidental meeting at Clifton's eating-house, in Butcher Row, a piece of old London pulled down in 1813. When Johnson had finished his dinner, and was leaving the room, Boswell followed him out, and, after some conversation, an appointment was made for a supper, that evening, at the Mitre. The event is described in the " Life " in enthusiastic terms : " The orthodox, High Church sound of the *Mitre*, the figure and manner of the celebrated *Samuel Johnson*, the extraordinary power and precision of his conversation, and the pride, arising from finding myself admitted as his companion, produced a variety of sensations, and a pleasing elevation of mind beyond what I had ever before experienced."

From the first meeting at Davies's house, Boswell had taken, what he called, "minutes of what passed."   The conversation, at the Mitre, was chiefly on literature, and Johnson's criticisms were very characteristic.   " Colley Cibber," he said, " was by no means a blockhead ; but, by arrogating to himself too much, he was in danger of losing that degree of estimation to which he was entitled." Speaking of the lines in one of Cibber's odes to the king :

> " Perch'd on the eagle's soaring wing,
>   The lowly linnet loves to sing "—

he said, "Sir, he had heard something of the fable of the wren sitting upon the eagle's wing, and he had applied it to a linnet." These remarks applied only to Cibber's poetry. Johnson had a high opinion of his powers as a dramatist.

"Goldsmith," he said, "is one of the first men we now have as an author." This remark, it must be noted, was made before the "Vicar of Wakefield" or the "Traveller" had been published. From the first, Gold-smith's genius had been discerned by Johnson, who was the only literary man of that day able thoroughly to appreciate his friend's extraordinary talent. This first supper at the Mitre was prolonged till between one and two in the morning, and a couple of bottles of port were finished, before the new friends left the tavern. Boswell had at length succeeded in forming the intimacy, so long the object of his wishes, an intimacy which was to give us one of the most delightful books in the world. It is needless to expatiate on the extraordinary merits of a work, which everybody has read, and everybody has praised. Lord Macaulay speaks of Boswell as "the first of biographers. He has no second. He has distanced all his competitors so decidedly that it is not worth while to place them. Eclipse is first, and the rest nowhere." Carlyle's description is equally enthusiastic : "Out of the fifteen millions," he writes, "that then lived, and had bed and board, in the British islands, this man (Boswell) has provided us a greater *pleasure* than any other individual at whose cost we now enjoy ourselves." There is a touching allusion to the subject in a letter from a lady, who writes to *The Spectator* of December 10, 1881, over the signature E. S. : "Many a time (my husband dining at an eating-house) did I eat only dry bread for dinner, all the while guarding and treasuring up a sovereign, given me by a cousin, and which I destined to the purchase of Boswell's 'Life of Johnson.' I had to wait five months 'ere opportunity favoured me, and not, until I had been some time at the Cape of Good Hope, did I triumphantly carry home my volumes. But when at last I held them, as my own, in my eager hands, what were exile, and poverty, and vexation, in comparison ? "

But the highest tribute, though an involuntary one, to the unapproachable superiority of Boswell's work, is that, notwithstanding its immense popularity, no one has ever tried to imitate it. There have been many biographies since, some by writers of great ability, but none of them have ventured to take Boswell as a model. His style is clearly recognized to be inimitable. It is not easy to describe the writer to whose work Johnson owes such a large portion of his fame. His character was exceedingly complex, and his good and bad qualities are strangely mixed. He was undoubtedly a man with "reverence for wisdom," as was clearly shown by his genuine admiration for Johnson, but there are records in the later part of his career which show that he was occasionally a sycophant, without even a pretence of self-respect. According to his own confession, he was a coward, and a constant regret of his life was that he had not been a soldier. At one time his friends feared his going over to the Roman Catholic faith, and, not long afterwards, he was professing a tendency to infidelity ; and in both cases he, perhaps believed himself to be sincere. When quite a boy, he fancied himself to be an adherent of the old cause, and drank King James's health when his father was toasting George III. ; but for the sake of a shilling, given to him by an uncle, he at once abandoned his Jacobite ideas. He called himself a Churchman and a Tory, and his dearest friend in the world was Jack Wilkes. A man of the most imperturbable good humour, and of a warm heart, he allowed himself to be childishly jealous of all those who were his rivals for Johnson's intimacy. Goldsmith is rarely mentioned in the " Life " without some sneering comment ; and his behaviour, after Johnson's death, to Mrs. Piozzi, was unmanly and ungenerous. No scruples prevented him from accepting the hospitality of Sir John Hawkins, whom he afterwards accused of down-right dishonesty, with little other cause but that Hawkins, in his biography, had mentioned him merely as Mr. James Boswell, without prefixing some epithet, like "the well-known " or " the celebrated," to his name.

He had undoubtedly a sincere belief in revealed religion, and tried to live in conformity with its precepts, but he had so little command over himself, that he was constantly indulging in excesses, which contrasted strangely with his pious inclinations. After these periods of debauch, he had fits of repentance, and his solemn vows of reformation and amendment gave him the same

6

serene satisfaction, which Pepys felt when he resolved to
give up his flirtations with Deb. Willett.   He was not a
good husband, though he had strong feelings of love and
respect for his wife.   His own relations, who were sin-
cerely attached to him, had so little pride in his literary
work that their first thought, after his death, was to burn all
his papers, which they could lay their hands on.   There
is no doubt as to his strict veracity, but he was constantly
blurting out truths which he had much better have left
unsaid.   His talents as a writer were appreciated by few
of his contemporaries, though his early work on Corsica
had exercised considerable influence on public opinion at
the time.   Sir George Trevelyan, in a note to " The
Early History of Charles James Fox," writes : " How real
was the effect produced by Boswell's narrative upon the
opinion of his countrymen may be gathered from the
unwilling testimony of those who regretted its influence,
and thought little of its author ; " and further on we read
" that Horace Walpole credited Boswell with having
procured Paoli his pension of a thousand a year from
the British exchequer."   But the members of that distinguished circle, which is chiefly known to us through
the pages of Boswell, could hardly be expected to
recognize his unrivalled qualities as a biographer.
The very weaknesses which made him—to many of
them, at least—an object of contempt and derision, were
of as much service to him as his literary qualities.   His
patience, his power of observation, his accuracy, his skill
in narrative, his dramatic power of arranging details, his
gift of discerning the good points of a story, and his
retentive memory were scarcely more valuable to him

in composing his "Life" than his strange candour, his meanness, his inordinate curiosity, and his ignorance of his own absurdities. His whole life was devoted to one object, and in that object he obtained success, such as in his wildest dreams he could never have anticipated.

Boswell was at last on terms of familiarity with his hero, and many pleasant evenings were passed, at which Goldsmith was often present. If Johnson appreciated Goldsmith's talents, the latter, one of the most warm-hearted and generous of mankind, was equally cordial in admiration of his friend's sincere benevolence; and he was, perhaps, alone, at that time, in his recognition of the human sympathy and kindness which were concealed by Johnson's rugged demeanour. "He has nothing of a bear but the skin," said Goldsmith; and on surprise being expressed at his kindness to some worthless character, Goldsmith's touching remark was, "He has now become miserable, and that ensures the protection of Johnson."

An account is given by Boswell of a supper, with Johnson and Goldsmith, at the Mitre. It is one of the biographer's early essays at reporting, and shows how well he was fitted for the task. The conversation turned on literary subjects, and mention was made of Dr. John Campbell, a voluminous author, now entirely forgotten, whose works enjoyed considerable popularity in their day. Johnson said that he used to go pretty frequently to Campbell's on a Sunday evening, till he began to consider that the shoals of Scotchmen who flocked about him might probably say, when anything of his was well done, "Ay, ay, he has learnt this of *Cawmell.*"

" Churchill's poetry," he observed, "had a temporary currency, only from its audacity of abuse, and being filled with living names, and that it would sink into oblivion."

Boswell hinted that Johnson was hardly a fair judge, as Churchill had attacked him violently.

"*Johnson.* Nay, sir, I am a very fair judge. He did not attack me violently, till he found I did not like his poetry ; and his attack on me shall not prevent me from continuing to say what I think of him from an apprehension that it may be ascribed to resentment. No, sir, I called the fellow a blockhead at first, and I will call him a blockhead still."

Speaking of periodical papers, he said that *The Connoisseur* wanted matter, and that *The World* was not much better.

On leaving the tavern, Johnson, as was his custom, went to drink tea with Miss Williams, who then had lodgings in Bolt Court. Goldsmith accompanied him, "strutting away," and exciting Boswell's envy by calling to him with an air of superiority, "I go to Miss Williams." But Boswell's personal intercourse with Johnson was now for a time to cease. By his father's desire, he was going to study at Utrecht, and he was accompanied by his "revered friend" as far as Harwich, where an affectionate parting took place.

"I hope, sir," said Boswell, "you will not forget me in my absence."

"*Johnson.* Nay, sir, it is more likely you should forget me."

In the early part of 1764 Johnson paid a pleasant visit to Langton, the country seat of the family of that name, in Lincolnshire. There was no one whose society delighted him more than that of Bennet Langton. His amiable disposition, his high Tory principles, and his love of learning made him a congenial companion, and his importance was increased in Johnson's eyes by the knowledge that he belonged to a good old family which had owned land in the county since the days of Henry II. Langton had come up to London, while still a boy, before going to the University, and had managed to be introduced to Johnson by Levett. The acquaintance was continued at Oxford, where Johnson was staying on a visit, when Langton was an undergraduate at Trinity. "I see your pupil sometimes," writes Johnson in 1758 to Dr. Thomas Warton, who was Langton's college tutor; "his mind is as exalted as his stature. I am half afraid of him, but he is no less admirable than formidable. He will, if the forwardness of his spring be not blasted, be a credit to you and to the University."

Miss Hawkins, in her memoirs, gives a description of Langton's personal appearance. "Oh, that we could sketch him," she writes, "with his mild countenance, his elegant features, and his sweet smile, sitting with one leg twisted round the other, as if fearing to occupy more space than was equitable." Miss Reynolds, in her anecdotes, tells us with what energy and fond delight Johnson expatiated on his (Langton's) praise, giving him "every excellence that nature could bestow, and every perfection that humanity could acquire." Langton died at Southampton in December, 1801, and is buried in the ancient church of St. Michael, where a marble tablet is erected

to his memory, with the following inscription, "Sit anima
mea cum Langtono." These words had been once used
by Johnson, when speaking of the certainty of his friend's
happiness in a future life, and no more beautiful epitaph
could have been chosen to place over his grave.

At one of his visits to Oxford, Johnson had met
Langton's friend, Topham Beauclerk, a great-grandson of
Charles II. and Nell Gywn. He was a man of dissipated
habits, but of too good taste and propriety to make any
parade of his vices, and Johnson was soon fascinated by
his high-bred manners and polished address. Beauclerk
had a remarkable gift of saying a good thing without
effort, and with a look of unconsciousness of its effect
which added immensely to the charm of his conversation.
He thoroughly understood Johnson, and was able to take
liberties with him, which no other person would have presumed to do. On one occasion, when staying with Beauclerk at Windsor, Johnson was enticed on a fine Sunday
morning to saunter about the churchyard while service was
going on, and at length laid down on one of the tomb-
stones. "Now, sir," said Beauclerk, "you are like Hogarth's
Idle Apprentice." When Johnson was granted a pension, Beauclerk addressed him with a happy, and perhaps
too appropriate, quotation, slightly altered from Shakespeare, " I hope you will now purge and live cleanly like a
gentleman."

Garrick, when he heard of this new friendship, said,
" What a coalition ! I shall have my old friend to bail
out of the round-house."

CHAPTER VI

THE most important event of the year 1764 was the formation of "The Club." "A tavern chair," Johnson once asserted, "was the throne of human felicity;" and a club in those days combined the freedom of a tavern with the advantage, not only of associating with friends, but with only those friends, who had been chosen for their social qualities. Johnson had formerly belonged to a society which met weekly at The King's Head, in Ivy Lane. Hawkins has given, in his "Life of Johnson," a most interesting account of its members, among whom were Hawkins himself, Samuel Dyer, Hawkesworth, and Johnson's dear friend, Bathurst. Hawkins and Dyer were afterwards members of the more famous "Club," and the latter was one of the numerous claimants put forward for the authorship of "Junius's Letters."

"The Club," as it was at first called, was formed at the suggestion of Reynolds, and the number of members was limited to nine, who met once a week at The Turk's Head, Gerrard Street. The original members were Reynolds, Johnson, Edmund Burke, Dr. Nugent (Burke's father-in-law), Langton, Goldsmith, Chamier, and Sir

John Hawkins. Garrick was not a member till 1773, and, later in the same year, Boswell was elected, though not, as he afterwards heard from Johnson, without considerable opposition. Charles James Fox, then only just twenty-five years of age, was elected a few months later, in the spring of 1774; but whether, as Sir George Trevelyan thinks, from respect for his elder companions, or from other causes, he took little part in the discussions. He does not appear to have been on very familiar terms with Johnson, who probably was never invited within the classic grounds of Holland House. Between Burke and Johnson there were warm feelings of regard and mutual respect. They first met at Garrick's house at a dinner party on Christmas Day, 1758, and notwithstanding the widest difference of opinion on political subjects, their friendship continued unaltered for more than a quarter of a century.

But there was one among that number with whom Johnson was on still closer terms. Reynolds was nearer his own age than any of the society with which he generally associated. Johnson had first met the great artist soon after his return from Italy, and their intimacy grew closer each year. "If I should lose you," writes Johnson to Reynolds in 1764, "I should lose almost the only man whom I call a friend." There was no other person with whom Johnson was able to feel himself on distinctly equal terms, and from him only Johnson ever cared to seek advice. When the offer was made of a pension, Reynolds was the first person consulted. There was no rivalry possible between the two men, each so eminent in different ways; and the last episode, in this interesting friendship, was when Johnson, from his death-bed, sent a messenger to Reynolds with three requests : to forgive him a small pecuniary debt; to read the Bible; and never to paint on a Sunday. Sir Joshua willingly promised to comply with his friend's wishes.

But Johnson's pen during this time was not entirely idle, and "The Traveller," published in December, was noticed by him in *The Critical Review* of January, 1765. "The Vanity of Human Wishes" had, as it was pointed out in the previous chapter, exercised considerable influence on Goldsmith's poetry, and the wiseacres of the time thought the greater part of his new work was written by Johnson, who had in reality contributed but nine lines. Two of these,

> " How small of all that human hearts endure,
> That part which laws or kings can cause or cure,"

might have been detected by an acute critic ; for the same sentiment is expressed in " Rasselas," when the astronomer speaks of "the task of a king who has the care only of a few millions, to whom he cannot do much good or harm." " The Traveller," one of the most exquisite gems in our language, obtained a wide popularity, and induced the publishers to bring out " The Vicar ot Wakefield," which its author had disposed of some time previously. The sale of Goldsmith's novel, as told by Boswell, is well known. " I received," said Johnson, " one morning a message from poor Goldsmith that he was in great distress, and as it was not in his power to come to me, begging that I would come to him as soon as possible. I sent him a guinea, and promised to come to him directly. I accordingly went, as soon as I was dressed, and found that his landlady had arrested him for his rent, at which he was in a violent passion. I perceived that he had already changed my guinea, and had got a bottle of Madeira and a glass before him. I put the cork in the bottle, desired he would be calm, and began to talk to him of the means by which he might be extricated. He then told me he had a novel ready for the press, which he produced to me. I looked into it, and saw its merit; told the landlady I should soon return; and, having gone to a bookseller, sold it for sixty pounds. I brought Goldsmith the money, and he discharged his rent, not without rating his landlady in a high tone for having used him so ill." There are other versions of the affair, which differ only in unimportant details. Johnson had often repeated the story, and some of his hearers may have retained imperfect recollections of the narrative. Mrs. Piozzi relates that the incident happened when Johnson was dining at her own table, but this account was written many years after the event took place, and her ideas on the subject had probably become confused. We know from a note, in Johnson's own writing, that he did not make the acquaintance of the Thrales till 1765, and the sale of Goldsmith's MS. took place, at the very latest, in 1764. Cumberland's account differs from the others in one amusing variation. He pretends that the landlady (most likely Mrs. Fleming, whose portrait Hogarth is said to have painted) offered to forgive Goldsmith's debt if he would take his creditor to wife, but this is probably a picturesque effort of the writer's imagination. A very interesting entry, referring to the subject, was, not

long ago, discovered in a ledger, marked "Account of
copies, their cost and value, 1764," which formerly
belonged to Mr. Benjamin Collins, of Salisbury, who
printed the first edition of the novel—"' Vicar of Wakefield,' 2 vols., 12 mo., ⅓ rd.   B. Collins, Salisbury, bought
of Dr. Goldsmith, the author, October 28, 1762.   £21."

This confirms Boswell's statement of the price received
by Goldsmith, viz., sixty pounds (which in those days
often meant guineas).   Johnson may have sold the work
for that sum, and brought home one-third of the price as
what Mrs. Piozzi calls "a temporary relief."   But it is for
Goldsmith's biographers to clear up these minor points
of difference in the story.

Johnson's acquaintance with the Thrales was commenced, as just stated, in 1765; and to it he was indebted,
as he afterwards acknowledged, for that "kindness which
soothed twenty years of a life radically wretched."   Mrs.
Thrale, when she was still a little girl, saw much of
Hogarth, who, in his picture of The Lady's Last Stake,
has given us a portrait of her, as she appeared in her fif-
teenth year.   "He was most anxious," she writes, "that I
should obtain the acquaintance and, if possible, the friendship of Dr. Johnson, whose conversation was, to the talk of
other men, like Titian's painting compared to Hudson's,
he said; 'but don't you tell people now,' continued he,
'for the connoisseurs and I are at war, you know; and
because I hate them, they think I hate Titian, and let
them!'"

Mrs. Thrale first saw Johnson on the second Thursday
of January, 1765, when he was taken by Murphy to dine
at Streatham, and was much pleased with his hosts and

their manner of living. " On the praises of Mrs. Thrale,"
writes Miss Reynolds, a trustworthy witness, " he used to
dwell with a peculiar delight, a paternal fondness, ex·
pressive of conscious exultation in being so intimately
acquainted with her.   One day, in speaking of her to
Mr. Harris, and expatiating on her various perfections,
the solidity of her virtues, the brilliancy of her wit, and
the strength of her understanding, he quoted some lines,
. . . and of these I retained but the last two :

> " ' Virtues of such a generous kind,
>   Good in the last recesses of the mind.' "

These praises of his " mistress," as Johnson used to
call her, were fully deserved. Her patience and womanly
kindness never varied, and he was always treated in her
house with the most assiduous attention and respect.
His health, about the time he made Mrs. Thrale's
acquaintance, was wretched, and was aggravated by the
morbid melancholy which he inherited from his father.
At one of her visits to Bolt Court, she found him in such
a distressing mental condition that she insisted on his
returning with her to Streatham, where, till their unfortunate rupture, he found the chief comfort of his life. There
is a delightful portrait by Reynolds of Mrs. Thrale, but it
appears to be rather too flattering, if we may judge of her
own description of herself; and the best likeness of her,
in the days when she was intimate with Johnson, is probably a faded miniature in the Dyce and Forster collection
at South Kensington.
    Among the events of this year (1765), was a visit to
Cambridge with Topham Beauclerk ; but a piece of

literary work, undertaken many years ago, now claimed
his attention. Johnson's edition of Shakespeare had
long been promised to the public, and many subscrip-
tions had been paid, of which all account had been lost;
but his indolence, and dislike to steady work and application, had hitherto prevented him from finishing the
uncongenial task. The subscribers were beginning to
lose patience. Churchill had made some unpleasant
allusions to the subject, and Foote had threatened to
caricature Johnson on the stage. Johnson quickly gave
the latter satirist to understand that, if he attempted
anything of the kind, he would receive severe chastise-
ment in the face of the audience, and the idea was
abandoned. But his friends felt that his credit was at
stake, and Reynolds, who had always great influence with
him, managed to obtain a definite promise that the work
should be completed by a certain time. It was at length
published in October of this year. The preface, though
the writer speaks too slightingly of the labours of his
predecessor, Theobald, is excellent, and contains admirable instructions for a commentator, which are not,
however, entirely carried out by their author. The
edition has never been much valued by students of
Shakespeare, and it is now seldom met with.

There were some thoughts, next year, of selling the old
house at Lichfield, and he writes to Lucy Porter on
January 14, 1766: "I was loth that Kitty should leave
the house till I had seen it once more, and yet for some
reasons I cannot well come during the session of Parliament. I am unwilling to sell it, yet scarcely know why."
The place was, however, not sold, and remained in John-

son's possession till his death, when it was bequeathed to some relatives of his father. Only quite recently the Corporation of Lichfield, in honour of their famous citizen, renewed to the present owner the lease granted first to Johnson's father, and afterwards to Johnson himself, of the part of the house abutting into Sadler's Lane, and a condition was made that the building should be kept in good repair.

Johnson was now established in Johnson's Court, Fleet Street, and from there he writes in March to Langton : "The Club subsists ; but we have the loss of Burke's company, since he has been engaged in public business, in which he has gained more reputation than perhaps any man at his first appearance gained before. . . . Burke is a great man by nature, and is expected soon to attain civil greatness. I am grown greater too, for I have maintained the newspapers these many weeks ; and, what is greater still, I have risen every morning since New Year's Day at about eight. . . . I wish you were in my new study ; I am now writing my first letter in it. I think it looks very pretty about me. Dyer is constant at the Club ; Hawkins is remiss : I am not over diligent ; Dr. Nugent, Dr. Goldsmith, and Mr. Reynolds are very constant."

Boswell was now in London, on his return from abroad, and we have full reports of Johnson's doings at this time. One evening Boswell and Goldsmith went to his house, and endeavoured to persuade him to come to supper at The Mitre, but the " big man," as Goldsmith called him, was unwilling to leave home, and they remained talking over a bottle of port wine, of which the host (then an abstainer) could not partake. Johnson was asked why his pen was now idle, and replied that he had dropped many of his old tastes.

"*Boswell.* But, sir, why don't you give us something in some other way?

"*Goldsmith.* Ay, sir, we have a claim upon you.

"*Johnson.* No, sir, I am not obliged to do any more. No man is obliged to do as much as he can do. A man is to have part of his life to himself. If a soldier has fought a good many campaigns, he is not to be blamed if he retires to ease and tranquility. A physician, who has practised long in a great city, may be excused if he retires to a small town and takes less practice. Now, sir, the good I can do by my conversation bears the same proportion to the good I can do by my writings that the practice of a physician retired to a small town does to his practice in a great city.

"*Boswell.* But I wonder, sir, you have not more pleasure in writing than in not writing.

"*Johnson.* Sir, you *may* wonder."

In the year 1767 Johnson had his celebrated interview with George III. Boswell's well-known account of this event is most graphic, and there can be no doubt of its accuracy, as it was submitted to the king for approval. Johnson acquitted himself with great propriety. "I found," he said, "that his Majesty wished I should talk, and I made it my business to talk." On one occasion, when he was narrating the particulars of the conversation at Sir Joshua Reynolds's house, and mentioned that his Majesty had praised his literary work, some one asked him whether he had replied to the compliment. "No, sir," answered Johnson, "when the king had said it, it was to be so—it was not for me to bandy civilities with my sovereign."

In the autumn he paid a long visit to Lichfield, and was present at the death of his mother's faithful old servant, Catherine Chambers. The affecting incident is noted in the "Prayers and Meditations."

"*Sunday, October* 18, 1767. Yesterday, October 17th, at about ten in the morning, I took my leave for ever of my dear old friend, Catherine Chambers, who came to live with my mother about 1724, and has but little parted from us since. She buried my father, my brother, and my mother. She is now fifty-eight years old. I desired all to withdraw, then told her that we were to part for ever; that, as Christians, we should part with prayer, and that I would, if she were willing, say a short prayer beside her. She expressed great desire to hear me, and held up her poor hands, as she lay in bed, with great fervour, while I prayed, kneeling by her, nearly in the following words:

"'Almighty and most merciful Father, whose loving-kindness is over all Thy works, behold, visit, and relieve this Thy servant, who is grieved with sickness; grant that the sense of her weakness may add strength to her faith and seriousness to her repentance; and grant that, by the help of Thy Holy Spirit, after the pains and labours of this short life, we may all obtain everlasting happiness, through Jesus Christ our Lord, for whose sake hear our prayers. AMEN. Our Father,' &c.

"I then kissed her. She told me that to part was the greatest pain she had ever felt, and that she hoped we should meet again in a better place. I expressed, with swelled eyes and great emotion of tenderness, the same hopes. We kissed and parted. I humbly hope to meet again and to part no more."

In 1768, and again in the following year, Boswell was in London. Some extracts from his description of a dinner party at his lodgings in 1769 afford a good specimen of Johnson's conversation, and of his biographer's skill in reporting :

"He honoured me with his company at dinner on the 16th of October, at my lodings in Old Bond Street, with Sir Joshua Reynolds, Mr. Garrick, Dr. Goldsmith, Mr. Murphy, Mr. Bickerstaff, and Mr. Thomas Davies. Garrick played round him with a fond vivacity, taking hold of the breasts of his coat and looking up in his face with a lively archness, complimented him on the good health which he seemed then to enjoy; while the sage, shaking his head, beheld him with a gentle complacency. One of the company, not being come at the appointed hour, I proposed, as usual upon such occasions, to order dinner to be served, adding, 'Ought six people to be kept waiting for one ?'

" 'Why, yes,' answered Johnson, with a delicate humanity, 'if the one will suffer more by your sitting down than the six will do by waiting.'

"Goldsmith, to divert the tedious minutes, strutted about, bragging of his dress, and, I believe, was seriously vain of it, for his mind was wonderfully prone to such impressions.

" 'Come, come,' said Garrick, 'talk no more of that, you are, perhaps, the worst—eh, eh !'

7

"Goldsmith was eagerly attempting to interrupt him, when Garrick went on, laughing ironically, 'Nay, you will always *look* like a gentleman, but I am talking of being well or *ill drest.*'

"'Well, let me tell you,' said Goldsmith, 'when my tailor brought home my bloom-coloured coat, he said, "Sir, I have a favour to beg of you. When anybody asks you who made your clothes,[1] be pleased to mention, John Filby, at 'The Harrow,' in Water Lane."'

"*Johnson*. Why, sir, that was because he knew the strange colour would attract crowds to gaze at it, and thus they might hear of him, and see how well he could make a coat even of so absurd a colour.

"After dinner our conversation first turned upon Pope.

"Johnson said 'his characters of men were admirably drawn, those of women not so well.' He repeated to us, in his forcible melodious manner, the concluding lines of 'The Dunciad.' While he was talking loudly in praise of those lines, one of the company [probably Boswell himself] ventured to say, 'Too fine for such a poem—a poem on what?'

"*Johnson* (with a disdainful look). Why, on *dunces*. It was worth while being a dunce then. Ah, sir, hadst *thou* lived in those days! It is not worth while being a dunce now when there are no wits.'

"Bickerstaff observed, as a peculiar circumstance, that Pope's fame was higher when he was alive than it was then. Johnson said his Pastorals were poor things, though the versification was fine. He told us, with high

[1] Mr. Filby's bill for the gorgeous raiment, of which the poet was so proud, is still in existence.

satisfaction, the anecdote of Pope's inquiring who was the author of his 'London,' and saying he will soon be *déterré.* He observed that in Dryden's poetry there were passages drawn from a profundity Pope could never reach. He repeated some fine lines on love by the former, which I have now forgotten, and gave great applause to the character of Zimri. Goldsmith said that Pope's character of Addison showed a deep knowledge of the human heart. Johnson said that the description of the temple in the 'Mourning Bride' was the finest poetical passage he had ever read; he recollected none in Shakespeare equal to it.

"'But,' said Garrick, all alarmed for the 'god of his idolatry,' 'we know not the extent and variety of nis powers. We are to suppose there are such passages in his works. Shakespeare must not suffer from the badness of our memories.'

"Johnson, diverted by this enthusiastic jealousy, went on with great ardour: 'No, sir, Congreve has nature' (smiling on the tragic eagerness of Garrick), but, composing himself, he added, 'Sir, this is not comparing Congreve on the whole with Shakespeare on the whole, but only maintaining that Congreve has one finer passage than any that can be found in Shakespeare. Sir, a man may have no more than ten guineas in the world, but he may have those ten guineas in one piece, and so may have a finer piece than a man who has ten thousand pounds; but then he has only one ten-guinea piece.'

"Talking of a barrister who had a bad utterance, some one (to rouse Johnson) wickedly said that he was unfortunate in not having been taught oratory by Sheridan.

"*Johnson.* Nay, sir, if he had been taught by Sheridan he would have cleared the room.

"Politics being mentioned, he said, 'This petitioning is a new mode of distressing Government, and a mighty easy one. I will undertake to get petitions either against quarter guineas or half guineas, with the help of a little hot wine. There must be no yielding to encourage this. The object is not important enough. We are not to blow up half-a-dozen palaces because one cottage is burning."

In 1770 Johnson wrote "The False Alarm." The whole country was at that time wild with excitement about the popular hero, John Wilkes, who had been three times expelled from the House of Commons, and on each occasion re-elected by his constituents. The pamphlet was written to prove that the House was acting strictly within its legal rights, and that a sentence of expulsion virtually amounted to exclusion. "A member of the House," Johnson sophistically argued, "cannot be cited for his conduct before any other court; and therefore, if the House cannot punish him, he may attack with impunity the rights of the people and the title of the king."

The pamphlet appeared on the 16th of January, and before the second edition was published in February, the Duke of Grafton had resigned, and Lord North became Prime Minister. It is impossible to consider without regret the career of that distinguished man, who, for thirteen years, from a mistaken feeling of loyalty to his sovereign, was employed in carrying out a policy, which his own judgment condemned, and which finally lost

England her American colonies. Lord North was not a great speaker, but his high courage, his abundant common sense, his ready wit, his equanimity of temper, supplied the higher qualities of statesmanship, and in other times he might have left behind him a reputation very different from that which he now occupies in history. During his long term of office he was confronted by an opposition that numbered among its members Charles James Fox, Burke, Dunning, and in later times the younger Pitt, and against this powerful array of orators he was able to hold his own.

Johnson's pamphlet was followed by many others on the same subject, but there was one which soon attracted universal attention. " The Thoughts on the Cause of the present Discontents " appeared on the 24th of April, and a second edition was issued on the 29th of the same month. It was published anonymously, but it was unnecessary to give the name of its author. There was no man living at that time, who could have written such a work, but Edmund Burke. It is a masterpiece of political writing. Its moderation, its impartial tone, its clear logic, and its powerful array of facts, made it impossible to answer, and it is still the best source of information for a knowledge of the history of that time.

"The False Alarm" was followed in 1771 by " Thoughts on the late Transactions respecting Falkland's Islands." The circumstances connected with the rival claims of England and Spain for the possession of these barren islands have long been forgotten, and probably few persons now know in what part of the world they are situated. But Johnson's pamphlet is still interesting from the excellent geographical and historical account of the place, and from the powerful invective which it contains against *Junius*, who remained, however, silent under the attack.

Johnson's health and spirits had much improved from his visits to the Thrales.   He mixed now a great deal in society, and made pretty frequent excursions to Lichfield. For some time he had meditated a journey to the Hebrides, and Boswell, who was in London in 1773, constantly pressed him to carry out the project.   It was in this year that the biographer dined at Johnson's house on Easter Day.   "I had gratified my curiosity much," he writes, "in dining with Jean Jacques Rousseau while he lived in the wilds of Neufchâtel.   I had a great curiosity to dine with Dr. Samuel Johnson in the dusky recesses of a court in Fleet Street.   I supposed we should scarcely have knives and forks, and only some strange, uncouth, and ill-drest dish.   But I found everything in very good order."   Foote, in allusion to Francis Barber, the negro servant, suggested that the dinner would consist of black broth, but the bill of fare, as given by Boswell, contained soup, a boiled leg of lamb and spinach, a veal pie, and a rice pudding.

Boswell left London in May, and, soon after his arrival in Scotland, wrote a pressing letter to Johnson, begging him to persevere in the visit to the Hebrides.   Mrs. Thrale, too, used her influence in the matter, and on the 14th of August Johnson arrived in Edinburgh.   The tour extended over two months, and must have been a strange experience to Johnson.   He had on some occasions to undergo serious hardships, and even dangers, but he derived no harm from his exertions, which for a man of sixty-four were pretty severe. On the very day after his arrival in London he wrote, "I came home last night without incommodity, danger, or weariness, and am ready to begin a new journey." Johnson's own account of the tour was not published till January, 1775. It is a plain, straightforward history of what he saw and did, related in characteristic language, and with not a few sarcastic sallies on the country and its inhabitants. It has no great literary value, but it may still be read with interest as a genuine description of the impressions which a visit to the wild scenes of the Hebrides produced on the mind of a man who thought that "the full tide of existence was at Charing Cross."

CHAPTER VII.

IN 1774 Johnson accompanied the Thrales on a Welsh tour, and on the way the party stopped at Lichfield, where he introduced his travelling companions to his step-daughter, Lucy Porter; to Peter Garrick, the brother of the great actor; to Mrs. Elizabeth Aston, the unmarried sister of his former flame, Molly Aston (now Mrs. Brodie); and to other residents of his native city. From Lichfield they went to Ashbourne, and passed a Sunday with Dr. Taylor. Boswell was not aware that Johnson during this time kept a diary, which has been since brought to light. After his death this interesting manuscript came into the possession of his servant, Francis Barber, and it was published by Mr. Duppa in 1816.

In the autumn of the following year Johnson went with the Thrales to Paris, and passed several weeks in visiting the sights of the place. A trip, too, was made to Versailles, where they saw the King and Queen at dinner, and Marie Antoinette must have made Mrs. Thrale very proud and happy by sending one of the gentlemen of the Court to ask the name of her daughter, Queenie Thrale.

Boswell was very anxious for Johnson to publish an

account of the visit to France, but he wisely refused to
comply with the suggestion. Such a book, he said,
would have an interest for Reynolds and the other
members of the " Club," but would contain nothing that
was not known already. One event, however, recorded
in the journal, which he kept during his stay in Paris,
deserves to be mentioned, on account of its literary
interest. At the English convent of the order of St.
Augustine, he had some conversation with the niece of
Arabella Fermor, who, under the name of "Belinda," is
immortalized in Pope's "Rape of the Lock." The lady
of the convent was not, however, proud of her aunt's
celebrity, and considered Pope's poem rather an insult
than an honour. Another incident, of no importance in
itself, has given rise to so much controversy that it cannot
be passed over in silence. A visit was paid to the house
of a Madame d'Argenson, and Johnson, like the *Spectator*
in Leonora's library, examined the books in the lady's
closet. Amongst them was the " Histoire du Prince
Titi," and on this Mr. Croker observes in a note, " ' The
history of Prince Titi ' was said to be the autobiography
of Frederick, Prince of Wales, but was probably written
by Ralph, his secretary. (See Parks' ' Royal and Noble
Authors,' vol. i. p. 171)." On this Lord Macaulay
remarks, " A more absurd note was never penned. The
history of Prince Titi to which Mr. Croker refers, whether
written by Prince Frederick or by Ralph, was *certainly
never published.* If Mr. Croker had taken the trouble to
read with attention the very passage in Parks' ' Royal
and Noble Authors ' which he cites as his authority, he
would have seen that the MS. was given up to the Govern-

ment. The history at which Johnson laughed was a very proper companion to the 'Bibliothèque des Fées,'—a fairy tale about good Prince Titi and naughty Prince Violent. Mr. Croker may find it in the 'Magasin des Enfans,' the first French book which the little girls of England read to their governesses."

Croker's original statement is not quite accurate. The history of Prince Titi was certainly *not* written by Ralph, but it was equally certain that the early portion of it was intended as an allegorical history of Frederick, Prince of Wales. Prince Titi's short allowance of money, his state of dependence on the will of his parents; the absurd but appropriate names given to King Ginguet and Queen Tripasse leave little doubt as to whom these characters were intended to personate. The ambassador, sent to the country of King Forteserre, is also clearly a portrait of Sir Robert Walpole's brother, who had been the representative of the English Court at Paris. He is described as an *échapé de Päisan*, he is *le frère du premier ministre*, and the narrator especially remarks on the ambassador's *rusticité naturelle*. It is impossible that this could refer to any one but old Horatio Walpole. The little volume was really the work of M. Paul de Themiseul, and Macaulay might have been satisfied with his triumph in pointing out Mr. Croker's error in describing Ralph as the author. But the brilliant essayist wished to give a little more finish to his satire, and talks of a fairy tale about good Prince Titi and naughty Prince Violent. Unfortunately there is no Prince Violent in the volume, and there is, at least, one very good reason for supposing that " Prince Titi " was at the time of its publication, supposed to be a genuine work. Two English versions of it immediately appeared, one of which was issued by the notorious Curll, and it is not very likely that he would have thought it worth while to publish a translation of a little girl's lesson book.

Johnson's literary work was now nearly finished. In 1774 he wrote "The Patriot," in which he endeavoured to warn the people of the difference between true and spurious patriotism. The former quality, he writes, "is not displayed by an acrimonious and unremitting opposition to the Court. A man may hate his king and not love his country. A person is not a patriot who disseminates discontent, and propagates reports of secret influence, of dangerous counsels, of violated rights, and encroaching usurpation. A true patriot is no lavish promiser; he undertakes not to shorten Parliaments; to repeal laws; or to change the mode of representation transmitted by our ancestors; he knows that futurity is not in his power, and that all times are not favourable to change."

The pamphlet, though it contained much that was undoubtedly true, was not a great success. It was followed in 1775 by "Taxation no Tyranny," an answer to the resolutions and address of the American Congress. The author asserts the supreme power of the community to require from its subjects such contributions as are necessary to the public safety or public prosperity. He ridicules the powers of the Americans to resist the will of the mother country, and declares that a Cornish Congress might meet at Truro, and, with equal right, address the other counties in the language of the

American patriots. There is much force and vigour in the pamphlet, but it is impossible to read it without feeling how unconscious was the writer of the great changes that were going on around him. It was the last time that his pen was employed for a political object, and the task was probably undertaken from a praiseworthy sense of duty.

In 1775 the University of Oxford conferred on Johnson a Doctor's degree. He had now attained a position of extraordinary dignity and reputation. His fame as a writer was at its zenith, much higher indeed than it is in our own day. His income was more than sufficient for his own wants, and for those of his numerous pensioners. His health was better than it had ever been before, and death had hardly begun to thin the circle of his intimate friends. It was in this year that he had the well-known controversy with Macpherson, the author of the English version of Ossian's poems. These were supposed to have been translated from ancient Erse manuscripts, but Johnson refused to believe it, and challenged the translator to produce the originals. The dispute at length became so fierce that Macpherson wrote with threats of personal violence. To this Johnson replied in the following letter, of which the original was, not many years ago, sold at the auction of Mr. Lewis Pocock, the owner of an unrivalled collection of "Johnsonian" MSS. :—

"Mr. James Macpherson,—I received your foolish and impudent letter. Any violence offered to me I shall do my best to repel, and what I cannot do for myself the law shall do for me. I hope I never shall be deterred from detecting what I think a cheat by the menaces of a ruffian.

"What would you have me retract? I thought your book an imposture; I think it an imposture still. For this opinion I have given my reasons to the public, which I here dare you to refute. Your rage I defy. Your abilities, since your Homer, are not so formidable; and what I hear of your morals, inclines me to pay regard, not to what you shall say, but to what you shall prove. You may print this if you will.

"SAM. JOHNSON."

Johnson provided himself with a stout cudgel, but Mr. Macpherson gave him no opportunity of using it.

Boswell arrived in London in March and remained till May, and we have accordingly a full account of Johnson during these months. Nothing is more remarkable in his career than the number and variety of the persons with whom he associated. One day he was dining with a nobleman, and on the morrow with Mrs. Gardiner, the wife of a tallow chandler, on Snow Hill. Among his acquaintance were persons of every sort and condition of life. One of his friends was Mrs. Abington, the most charming comedian of her time, who seems to have enjoyed a very exceptional position, and to have been intimate with some of the great ladies of the day. Her taste was unrivalled in all matters of dress, and her opinions on this important subject were accepted as law. She was a universal favourite, both with the public and in private life. The fastidious Horace Walpole had a great admiration for her acting, and, in defiance of all his usual regulations, gave her orders for admission to Strawberry Hill, with leave to bring as many friends as she liked. She frequently sat to Reynolds, and we know of at least four portraits of her by that great painter. At her particular request, Johnson—though he confessed he could neither see nor hear—attended her benefit this year at Drury Lane. Reynolds had taken forty places in the front boxes, and filled them with his friends, among whom was Johnson, "wrapped up in grave abstraction." A fortnight afterwards he supped with a fashionable company at Mrs. Abington's house, and next day, when dining at the Thrales, he humorously pretended to excite the jealousy of his hostess by praising Mrs. Abington's jelly. There are many more dinners at that time recorded in the lively pages of Boswell, and in the autumn Johnson made the journey to Paris, which has been already described.

In 1776 Johnson moved into No. 8, Bolt Court,[1] which he occupied till his death. The house, and its strange collection of inhabitants, have often been described, and sometimes with unnecessary exaggeration. Casual visitors found it little different from other households of the same class. The drawing-room was well furnished with a stout mahogany table and chairs; friends were occasionally entertained, and had no reason to complain of the fare, or of the manner in which it was served. Boswell had at first a room, where he could occasionally sleep when he remained till late talking with Johnson, but it was afterwards

---

[1] The house still (1887) remains in the same condition, as when lived in by Johnson.

given up to Mrs. Desmoulins and her daughter. These
ladies shared it with Miss Carmichael, a strange creature
whom Johnson generally called "Poll." Blind Mrs.
Williams had her own apartment. Levett lived in an
attic, and sometimes a poor waif and stray would find a
night's lodging on his floor. Barber and his wife must
have slept somewhere, and there was a female servant,
Mrs. White, to whom Johnson left a legacy of £100.
There was, as might be expected, much contention
between these strange companions. Mrs. Williams had
a great dislike to the black servant, Barber, and was constantly making sarcastic allusions to the money which
had been spent on his education. When there was
company, Mrs. Williams and Mrs. Desmoulins took the
head of the table by turns. One day, on the occasion
of some dispute as to which of the two ladies should
preside, Mr. John Nichols ventured to observe that this
time Roxana should take the place of Statira. "Yes, sir,"
said Johnson, "but in my family it has never been
decided which is Roxana and which is Statira." There
was one point of union however between Mrs. Williams
and Mrs. Desmoulins, and that was their common dislike
for Miss Carmichael. Johnson told Miss Burney that
general anarchy prevailed in the kitchen, of which Mrs.
Desmoulins had the nominal management. There was no
jack, and Mr. Thrale asked how they managed without.

"*Johnson.* Small joints, I believe, they manage with
a string, and larger are done at the tavern. I have some
thoughts (with a profound gravity) of buying a jack,
because I think a jack is some credit to a house.

"*Thrale.* Well, but you'll have a spit too?

" *Johnson.* No, sir, no, that would be superfluous, for we shall never use it, and if a jack is seen a spit will be presumed."

While Johnson was living at Streatham it was his custom, Mrs. Piozzi relates in her "Anecdotes," to return to Bolt Court every Saturday and remain till Monday night, so as to give his pensioners three good dinners, "treating them with the same, or perhaps more ceremonious, civility than he would have done by as many people of fashion."

In March, 1776, the year after the excursion to Paris, Johnson, accompanied by Boswell, with whom he delighted to travel, made a short visit to Oxford, and the biographer learnt a good deal about his friend's academical career. After a few pleasant days, the journey was continued to Birmingham, where they met Johnson's former comrade, Hector, from whom Boswell obtained some particulars of Johnson's schooldays. Here, too, he saw Mrs. Careless, Hector's sister, one of Johnson's early flames. "On our return from Mr. Boulton's," writes Boswell, "Mr. Hector took me to his house, where we found Johnson sitting placidly at tea with his *first love,* who, though now advanced in years, was a genteel woman and well bred." Another friend at Birmingham was Mr. Lloyd, "one of the people called Quakers," who was probably a relative of Olivia Lloyd, to whom Johnson wrote verses when a boy at Stourbridge school. At Mr. Lloyd's house, on the north side of New Square, which still (1887) stands, very little changed since that time, the party were hospitably received at dinner, but an untoward event occurred, which for a time rather spoilt the harmony of the entertainment.   Boswell, who knew Johnson's strong feeling against all forms of dissent, imprudently asked to see a copy of Barclay's " Apology."

"Johnson laid hold of it, and the chapter on baptism happening to open, Johnson remarked, 'He says there is neither precept nor practice for baptism in the Scriptures; that is false.' Here he was the aggressor, by no means in a gentle manner, and the good Quakers had the advantage of him, for he had read negligently, and had not observed that Barclay speaks of *infant* baptism, which they calmly made him perceive." This identical copy of Baskerville's edition of Barclay's " Apology " is still preserved in the family. One of the company objected to the observance of "days, and months, and years." Johnson's answer was extremely happy, " The church," he said, " does not superstitiously observe days merely as days, but as memorials of important facts: Christmas might be kept as well upon one day of the year as another, but there should be a stated day for commemorating the birth of our Saviour."

Boswell wished to sleep at Birmingham, and get some more information from Hector, but Johnson was anxious to reach his native city, and they started that same evening. At Lichfield they put up at the Three Crowns, an old-fashioned tavern, next door to the house where Johnson was brought up. The Three Crowns is still (1887) practically unchanged, and retains an interesting piece of eighteenth-century furniture, which is called " Dr. Johnson's chair." The old inn does a respectable business, though it is not so large or important as the George, supposed to be the scene of

8

Farquhar's famous comedy, "The Beaux Stratagem;" or
the Swan, where Johnson stayed with the Thrales in
1774.   On the morning after their arrival Boswell was
introduced to Lucy Porter, then "an old maid with much
simplicity of manner;" and he also met Peter Garrick, who
bore a strong resemblance to his celebrated brother.   There
appeared to be very little business going in the place,
and Boswell remarked "that the inhabitants were an
idle set."   "Sir," answered Johnson, "we are a city of
philosophers; we work with our heads, and make the
boobies of Birmingham work for us with their hands."
In the evening they drank tea with Peter Garrick, where
they found Molly Aston's unmarried sister.   She and
another sister, Mrs. Gastrell, lived just outside the city,
on Stow Hill, in neighbouring houses, which still remain.
It was during this visit that Boswell first saw Anna Seward,
the poetess, with whom, after Johnson's death, he was to
have a very angry controversy.   She was, as mentioned
in a former chapter, a daughter of Dr. Hunter, who had
been headmaster of the Grammar School.

At Lichfield Johnson was much shocked by the news
of the death of Mr. Thrale's only son, and determined
to hasten his return to London.   On March 26th, the
travellers were conveyed to Ashbourne in Dr. Taylor's
"large roomy post-chaise, drawn by four stout, plump
horses, and driven by two steady, jolly postillions."
Boswell was again able to make substantial additions to
his materials for the "Life," and was much pleased at
seeing the cordial meeting between Johnson and his old
schoolfellow.   On the second day of their visit some
of the neighbours joined the party at dinner, and Boswell

was unlucky enough to draw upon himself a severe reproof
from his "illustrious friend." The company was discussing the advantages of fine clothes, and the guests must have
been a good deal amused at the following dialogue :—

"*Johnson.* No, sir, fine clothes are good only as
they supply the want of other means of procuring respect.
Was Charles the Twelfth, think you, less respected for
his worn blue coat and his black stock? and you find
the King of Prussia dresses plain, because the dignity of
his character is sufficient.

"*Boswell.* Would not *you*, sir, be the better for
velvet and embroidery?

"*Johnson.* Sir, you put an end to all argument when
you introduce your opponent himself."

After dinner the return journey was commenced. At
Leicester Johnson heard of the death of his schoolfellow, Dr. James, and said : "Since I have set out on
this journey I have lost an old friend and a young one,
Dr. James and poor Harry Thrale."

On his arrival in London he at once went to the
Thrales, and appears to have been rather disconcerted at
finding them on the point of starting for Bath, though
they knew that he had shortened his excursion in order
to come to them in their distress.

An amusing incident in Johnson's life occurred this year
(1776). In his political pamphlets, "The False Alarm" and
"The Patriot," he had treated John Wilkes with great
severity, and had always expressed strong disapproval
both of his public and private principles. "Two men
more different," writes Boswell, "would perhaps not be
selected out of all mankind," and the biographer was

now anxious to bring together these opposite characters.
Mr. Dilly, the bookseller of the Poultry, a Dissenter and
a Whig, had asked Boswell to meet his friend Wilkes at
dinner. The invitation was accepted, and Boswell requested permission to bring Johnson. Mr. Dilly was
aghast at the proposal. "What," he said, "with Mr.
Wilkes? not for the world; Dr. Johnson would never
forgive me." But Boswell promised he would arrange
the affair, and be answerable for anything that might
happen. The first stage in the negotiation, and perhaps
the most difficult, was to convey the invitation to
Johnson. If a direct proposal had been made to meet
Jack Wilkes at dinner, Johnson, would almost certainly,
as Boswell suggests, have flown into a violent passion,
and refused in pretty strong language. The diplomatic
manner, in which the affair was brought about, is very
amusing, and the dialogue on this occasion must be
quoted from Boswell's " Life " :

" *Boswell.* Mr. Dilly, sir, sends his respectful compli-
ments, and would be happy if you would do him the
honour to dine with him on Wednesday along with me,
as I must soon go to Scotland.

" *Johnson.* Sir, I am obliged to Mr. Dilly, I will wait
on him.

" *Boswell.* Provided, sir, I suppose, that the company
which he is to have is agreeable to you.

" *Johnson.* What do you mean, sir? What do you
take me for ! Do you think I am so ignorant of the
world as to imagine that I am to prescribe to a gentleman
what company he is to have at his table ?

" *Boswell.* I should not be surprised to find Jack
Wilkes there.

" *Johnson.* And if Jack Wilkes *should* be there what is that *to me*, sir ? "

On the appointed day, May 15th, Boswell called at Bolt Court to accompany Johnson to the dinner, but found he had forgotten the engagement, and had promised to dine at home with Miss Williams. The lady was at first very unwilling to let the doctor go, but finally yielded to the solicitations of Boswell and gave her consent. As soon as Miss Williams was appeased, Frank Barber was ordered to bring a clean shirt, and in a few minutes Johnson was dressed and seated in a hackney coach on the road to Mr. Dilly's house. On entering the drawing-room he found that many of the company were strangers, and he whispered to his host inquiring their names. " And who is the gentleman in lace ? " he at last asked. " Mr. Wilkes, sir," was the reply. This rather startled him, and he took up a book, on which for some minutes he kept his eyes fixed. He recollected, however, his rebuke to Boswell for supposing that he could be disconcerted by strange company, and was quite composed by the time dinner was announced. Of this interesting evening Boswell gives an excellent account, of which some idea may be formed by the following extracts :—

" Mr. Wilkes found himself next to Dr. Johnson, and behaved to him with so much attention and politeness that he gained upon him insensibly. No man eat more heartily than Johnson, or loved better what was nice and delicate. Mr. Wilkes was very assiduous in helping him to some fine veal. ' Pray give me leave, sir,—it is better here—a little of the brown—some fat, sir—a little of the stuffing, some gravy.—Let me have the pleasure of giving you some butter.—Allow me to recommend a squeeze of this orange ; or the lemon perhaps may have more zest.' ' Sir, sir ; I am obliged to you, sir,' cried Johnson, bowing and turning his head to him with a look for some time of 'surly virtue,' but in a short while of complacency. Foote being mentioned, Johnson said : 'He is not a good mimic. . . . One species of wit he has in an eminent degree—that of escape. You drive him into a corner with both hands, but he's gone, sir, when you think you have got him, like an animal that jumps over your head. Then he has a great range for wit ; he never lets truth stand between him and a jest, and he is sometimes mighty coarse. Garrick is under many restraints from which Foote is free.'

"*Wilkes.* Garrick's wit is more like Lord Chesterfield's.

"*Johnson.* The first time I was in company with Foote was at Fitzherbert's. Having no good opinion of the fellow I was resolved not to be pleased. I went on eating my dinner pretty sullenly, affecting not to mind him. But the dog was so very comical that I was obliged to lay down my knife and fork, throw myself back upon my chair and fairly laugh it out. No, sir, he was irresistible. . . .

" Mr. Arthur Lee mentioned some Scotch who had taken possession of a barren part of America, and wondered why they should choose it.

"*Johnson.* Why, sir, all barrenness is comparative. The Scotch would not know it to be barren.

" *Boswell.* Come, come, he is flattering the English.

" *Johnson* (to Mr. Wilkes). You must know, sir, I lately took my friend Boswell and showed him genuine

civilized life in an English provincial town. I turned
him loose at Lichfield, my native city, that he might
see for once civility; for you know he lives among
savages in Scotland and rakes in London.

"*Wilkes.* Except when he is with grave, sober,
decent people like you and me.

"*Johnson* (smiling). And we, ashamed of him."

After dinner the company was joined by Mrs. Knowles,
a Quaker lady famous for copying pictures in needle-
work. Croker asserts she was by no means attractive,
but the engraved portrait of her represents an extremely
pretty woman.[1] Johnson seems to have been rather
smitten with the lady's appearance. Boswell writes:
"Mr. Wilkes held a candle to show a fine print of a
beautiful female figure which hung in the room, and
pointed out the elegant contour of the bosom with the
finger of an arch connoisseur. He afterwards, in a conversation with me, waggishly insisted that all the time Johnson
showed visible signs of a fervent admiration of the corres-
ponding charms of the fair Quaker." Boswell accompanied Johnson home to his house, and was pleased to
hear him tell Mrs. Williams that he had had a very
pleasant evening.

Two years afterwards, in 1778, Johnson again met
Mrs. Knowles at Mr. Dilly's, and an illustration, which
she made use of in discussing a question of Divinity,
elicited Johnson's warm praise. The conversation had
taken a theological turn, and Johnson argued that Chris-

[1] When Molly Morris of Rageby, before her marriage, she was
known as "*the beauty of Staffordshire.*" She survived her husband,
Dr. Knowles, for many years, and died February, 4, 1807, aged 80.

tianity recommended universal benevolence. "Surely, madam," he said, "your sect must approve of this, for you call men *friends*."

"*Mrs. Knowles*.   We are commended to do good to all men, but especially to them who are of the household of faith !

"*Johnson*.   Well, madam, the household of faith is wide enough.

"*Mrs. Knowles*.   But, Doctor, our Saviour had twelve apostles, yet there was *one* whom he *loved*.   John was called 'the disciple whom Jesus loved.'

"*Johnson* (with eyes sparkling benignantly).   Very well indeed, madam ; you have said very well.

"*Boswell*.   A fine application.   Pray, sir, had you ever thought of it?"

"*Johnson*.   I had not, sir."

Mention was made of the Rev. Mr. Mason's prosecution of Mr. Murray, the bookseller, for having inserted in a collection of "Gray's Poems" fifty lines of which Mr. Mason still had the copyright.   Johnson expressed his strong disapprobation of the poet's conduct, and added, "Mason's a Whig.

"*Mrs. Knowles* (who had not distinctly heard).   What, a prig, sir ?

"*Johnson*.   Worse, madam, a Whig.   But he's both."

A very angry controversy now rose between Mrs. Knowles and Johnson, in which the former decidedly gained the advantage.   She mentioned that Miss Jane Harry, a young lady to whom Johnson had shown kindness, had joined the Society of Friends, and in the gentlest manner entreated the Doctor's indulgence for his young friend.

'*Johnson* (frowning very angrily). Madam, she is an odious wench. . . . She knew no more of the Church which she left and that which she embraced, than she did of the difference between the Copernican and Ptolemaic systems.

" *Mrs. Knowles.* She had the New Testament before her.

" *Johnson.* Madam, she could not understand the New Testament, the most difficult book in the world, for which the study of a lifetime is required.

" *Mrs. Knowles.* It is clear as to essentials.

" *Johnson.* But not as to controversial points.

" *Mrs. Knowles.* Must we, then, go by implicit faith ?

" *Johnson.* Why, madam, the greatest part of our knowledge is implicit faith. . . .

" He then," said Boswell, "rose again into passion, and attacked the young proselyte in the severest terms of reproach."

Mrs. Knowles published a full account[1] of the controversy with Dr. Johnson, and it is easy to see that Boswell had good reason for not giving fuller details. He was much too conscientious and honourable to make the least alteration in any of the conversations which he reported ; but he probably thought it allowable to condense considerably on certain occasions.

[1] It appeared in *The Gentleman's Magazine* for June, 1791, and was afterwards issued as a pamphlet in 1799.

CHAPTER VIII

GOLDSMITH had died in 1774, and Johnson had announced his death in a letter to Boswell of the 4th of July of that year.

"Of poor, dear Dr. Goldsmith there is little to be told more than the papers have made public. He died of a fever, I am afraid more violent by uneasiness of mind. His debts began to be heavy, and all his resources were exhausted. Sir Joshua is of opinion that he owed not less than two thousand pounds. Was ever poet so trusted before?"

It had at first been contemplated to give him a public funeral, but the design was abandoned, and he was buried in the graveyard of the Temple Church with such privacy that the site of his grave is now not known. Reynolds had at this time (1776) originated the idea of a monument in the Abbey, and the epitaph was written by Johnson. A good deal of opposition was made to its being in Latin, and some members of the "Club," including Burke, Gibbon, Sheridan, and Reynolds, drew up a remonstrance, in the form of a round robin, to the following effect: "We, the Circumscribers, having read with great pleasure, an intended epitaph for the monument of Dr. Goldsmith, which, considered abstractedly, appears to be, for elegant composition, and masterly style, in every respect worthy of the pen of its learned author, are yet of opinion that the character of the deceased as a writer, particularly as a poet, is perhaps not delineated with all the exactness which Dr. Johnson is capable of giving it ; we therefore, with deference to his superior judgment, humbly request that he would at least take the trouble of revising it, and of making such additions and alterations as he shall think proper upon a farther perusal ; but if we might venture to express our wishes, they would lead us to request that he would write the epitaph in English rather than in Latin, as we think that the memory of so eminent an English writer ought to be perpetuated in the language to which his works are likely to be so lasting an ornament, which we also know to have been the opinion of the late Doctor himself." But the sturdy old scholar refused " to disgrace the walls of Westminster Abbey with an English inscription," and the Latin original was, accordingly, placed on the tablet beneath the medallion of the poet's head.

In 1777, Johnson undertook a congenial work, for which he was in every way fitted, and which may still be read with delight and interest. The first four volumes appeared, in 1779, as the " Prefaces, Biographical and Critical, of the most eminent of the English Poets," and the series was completed in 1781. These " Prefaces " were afterwards published as " Lives of the English Poets," but the former title is more correct. The " Lives," admirable in their own way, are not so much biographies as critical essays. Few attempts are made to give exact details, and in some cases, where information was supplied, Johnson neglected to make use of it. The " Life of Savage," already referred to, is undoubtedly the best of the series, but a critic once said of it that it contained only one date, and that date incorrect. This is a manifest exaggeration, but it is certainly a matter of regret, that, at a time, when, for some of the " Lives," it was possible to procure most valuable information, no such attempt was made.

In our own day, considerable surprise would be expressed if the writer of a biography of Congreve were bold enough to say—"Of his (Congreve's) plays I cannot speak distinctly, for since I inspected them many years have passed ;" or whose remarks on Congreve's first novel, " Incognita," were limited to a candid confession, " It is praised by the biographers, I would rather praise it than read it."

But Johnson's memory was so retentive, and his acquaintance with English literature so extensive, that he was able, from his previous knowledge, to give an excellent account of most of the works which he criticises, and his remarks are often of the greatest interest and value. The strange paradoxes, in which he indulged in his ordinary conversation, appear rarely in the " Lives," and, in many cases, where he had conceived a strong prejudice against the works of certain writers, he carefully discriminates between the merits and defects of their separate productions. He had no admiration for Gray, but he does full justice to his " Elegy," of which he says, " Had Gray often written thus, it had been vain to blame, and useless to praise him ;" and on one occasion,

in discussing " The Bard," he acknowledged the extraordinary beauty of the two lines—

> " Tho' fann'd by Conquest's crimson wing
> They mock the air with idle state."

There are probably many critics now who, with a hearty
admiration for Gray's exquisite choice of language, and
the simple beauty of his style, agree with Johnson that
he was a " mechanical poet."

Charles James Fox and many others, among whom
was William Cowper, the author of " The Task," complained bitterly of Johnson's treatment of their favourite
authors. Some of the " Lives," especially those of Gray,
Milton, and Lyttelton, were commented on with great
severity, but this feeling of anger appears difficult to understand. The biographical portion of the work contains
nothing to offend any sensibilities, and even in the case
of Milton, whose political principles Johnson detested,
great veneration is expressed for his abilities and his
personal character. The sublimity of the " Paradise
Lost" is admitted, but Johnson could hardly be expected
to praise pastoral poetry, which he disliked, especially
when accompanied by mythological imagery. It seemed
to his strong common-sense mere absurdity for a poet to
assume the character of a shepherd, and address another
poet in a similar disguise : " What image of tenderness,"
he writes, in speaking of " Lycidas," "can be excited by
these lines ?

> ' We drove afield, and both together heard
> What time the gray fly winds her sultry horn,
> Battening our flocks with the fresh dews of night.'

We know that they never drove afield, and that they had no flocks to batten; and though it be allowed that the representation may be allegorical, the true meaning is so uncertain, and remote, that it is never sought, because it cannot be known when it is found."

A small minority still agree with Johnson's want of appreciation of "Lycidas," which is deservedly considered as one of the gems of our language. Only quite recently a poet of some University reputation, Sir Francis Doyle, confessed in his "Reminiscences" that he was not able to admire "Lycidas."

While preparing Lord Lyttelton's biography, Johnson had addressed a polite letter to that nobleman's brother, stating how glad he should be, if some member of the family would undertake the narrative portion of the memoir. The offer was courteously refused, but it absolves Johnson from any intention of ill-feeling or spite.

In 1778 Johnson made the acquaintance of Miss Burney, who in August was staying on her first visit to Streatham; and in her "Diary," published many years later, we have some lively sketches of Johnson, taken from a different point of view to those from which he is generally presented. He at once formed a warm friendship for "little Burney," and this was most cordially returned. Her novel of "Evelina" had appeared in the preceding January. It was published by an unknown firm, and at first attracted little attention, but it made its way by degrees, and at length achieved a success, almost unprecedented in the history of literature. Reynolds had been so interested in its contents that he had offered fifty pounds to know the name of the author; Edmund

Burke had sat up a whole night to read it; Johnson pro-
tested there were passages in it that would do honour to
Richardson; Daddy Crisp, the great friend of the Burney
family, had declared that in some respects it was superior
to Fielding. These flattering comments are related by
the lady herself, but there is no doubt of their authenti-
city, though they must cause considerable surprise to a
generation which knows something of the novels of Jane
Austen, and of George Eliot. The work was conceived
in an entirely new style, and the writer is entitled to very
high praise for her courage in striking out a fresh line
in fiction, though the story itself is little superior, either in
design or execution, to those with which the readers of
The Family Herald, and other modern periodicals, are
familiar. But Macaulay, in his well-known essay on
" Madame D'Arblay," has mentioned " Evelina " in enthusiastic terms, and it will probably be known, at least
in name, as long as any work of that class in our language. It can scarcely be thought surprising that Miss
Burney should feel elated at finding herself treated
with such extraordinary adulation, but it would have
been wiser if, in her diary and letters, she had been
a little more reticent on the subject. Johnson,
however, was delighted with her, and they remained
till his death on the most intimate and affectionate terms. He talked to her with the most delicate
flattery; he wrote to her; he tried to teach her Latin;
and in his last illness, when he was too unwell for an
interview, he sent the kindest messages, and begged for
her prayers.

Miss Burney's name is rarely mentioned by Boswell,

whom she had deeply offended by her refusal to lend him her letters from Johnson, or to give any information on the subject. One of the most amusing passages in her " Diary," is the account of her interview with the biographer at Windsor in 1790. He met her at the gates of the choir, and begged some of "her choice little notes of the Doctor. . . . Grave Sam," he said, "and great Sam, and solemn Sam, and learned Sam, all these he has appeared over and over. . . . I want to show him as gay Sam, agreeable Sam, pleasant' Sam ; so you must help me with some of his beautiful billets to yourself." Miss Burney tried to evade his requests, but he was importunate, and followed her up to the castle gate, where he insisted on reading to her a letter from Johnson to himself. A crowd began to assemble, and the king and queen were seen approaching from the Terrace. Miss Burney made her tormentor a hasty apology, and fled to her apartments.

Mr. Croker was equally unable to obtain any assistance from Madame d'Arblay (as Miss Burney had then become). There can be little doubt that her refusal was wrong, and it was probably dictated by that morbid vanity which, to the last, disfigured her many good qualities. Johnson, when questioned on the subject, had expressly declared that there could be no objection to publishing a man's letters after his death ; and Madame d'Arblay must have seen this statement in Boswell's " Life." An interesting mention of the lady occurs in one of Disraeli's recently-published letters to his sister. "'Contarini,' he writes, seems universally liked, but moves slowly. The staunchest admirer I have in London, and the most discerning appreciator of 'Contarini,' is old Madame d'Arblay. I have a long letter, which I will show you. Capital !"

There were many of Johnson's friends, besides Miss Burney, in the Streatham circle of whom we hear very little in Boswell's work. There was Mrs. Cholmondeley, the sister of Peg Woffington, whom Johnson must have known for many years. She had a good deal of the family cleverness, and joined so much sound sense to her more brilliant qualities, that Miss Burney declared "she would bring about a union between wit and judgment." There was also the beautiful Mrs. Crewe, the friend of Burke and of Charles James Fox; and her sister, Mrs. Greville, whose "Ode to Indifference" was much admired in its time; and there were others, whose names we only learn by some chance mention. But the most interesting member of the coterie was Sophy Streatfield, generally known as "S. S.," one of the most lovely women of her day; and Miss Burney affected to be "really astonished when Mrs. Thrale hinted at my becoming a rival to Miss Streatfield in the Doctor's good graces." Johnson had declared that the latter was a sweet creature, and he loved her much, but that Burney wrote a better letter. Miss Streatfield, though she was allowed, even by her rivals, to be a woman of strict principles, was probably the most accomplished coquette that ever breathed. Her special admiration was for men who were tall and thin, but no one of the male sex was safe from her attentions. Old and young, married and single, noblemen, reverend—very reverend—and even right reverend divines, were each, at times, the victim of her fascinations. Nobody was supposed to be so pretty,

9

when she·cried, as Miss Streatfield; and one of her
charms was the strange power of shedding tears whenever she wished.

"Yes, do cry a little, Sophy," said Mrs. Thrale to her
on one occasion when she wished this uncommon art to
be displayed to some guests; "pray do! Consider now,
you are going to-day, and it is very hard if you won't cry
a little; indeed, S. S., you ought to cry."

"Now for the wonder of wonders," adds Miss Burney.
"When Mrs. Thrale, in a coaxing voice, suited to a baby,
had run on some time—while all of us, in laughter,
joined in the request—two crystal tears came into the
soft eyes of the S. S., and rolled gently down her
cheeks."

Besides her beauty, however, she had considerable
intellectual attainments. She was a woman of culture,
an excellent Greek scholar, and had published an
edition of the classics. At Chiddingstone, the picturesque family seat in Kent, there is still (1887) an
extremely beautiful miniature of Sophy Streatfield, attributed to Cosway; and on the library shelves, very properly,
appear handsomely-bound copies of her classics. Her
flirtations were, unfortunately, carried on a little too long,
and the man, whom she really loved, proved at last to be
faithless. Colonel H. D. Streatfield, the present head of
the family, has a dim remembrance of the S. S. as a
feeble, withered old lady crossing over the bridge between
the pleasure ground and the churchyard, on her way to
the morning service. She died unmarried on the 30th
November, 1835, in the eighty-first year of her age.

An epigrammatic description of one of Mrs. Thrale's

parties is given in a letter written by her about this time to Fanny Burney : " Yesterday I had a conversazione. Mrs. Montague was brilliant in diamonds, solid in judgment, critical in talk. Sophy smiled, Piozzi sung, Pepys panted with admiration, Johnson was good-humoured, Lord John Clinton attentive, Dr. Bowdler lame, and my master not asleep. Mrs. Ord looked elegant, Lady Rothes dainty, Mrs. Davenant dapper, and Sir Phillip's curls were all blown about by the wind. Mrs. Byron rejoices that her Admiral and I agree so well; the way to his heart is connoisseurship, it seems, and for a background and contour who comes up to Mrs. Thrale you know."

A class of persons much less agreeable than those, just referred to, were the needy authors with whom Johnson had much intercourse. His kindness in assisting his poorer professional brethren was so well known that there was scarcely a day when his opinion was not asked about some literary production. Poets, historians, dramatists, and writers in every branch of learning, brought their manuscripts for his correction and approval ; and, though he hated the task, he was always ready to help them.

On one occasion, when Boswell, in 1779, had just arrived in London, he went to Bolt Court, and found Johnson sitting over his breakfast with Mrs. Desmoulins, Levett, and a clergyman who had come to submit some poems for revision. The doctor was reading a translation of " The Carmen Seculare " of Horace, and when he had finished, the author wished to know his opinion, and asked " if upon the whole it was a good translation." Johnson, with great diplomatic skill, and with strict

adherence to truth, spared the writer's feelings by saying:
"Sir, I do not say that it may not be made a very good
translation." "A printed 'Ode to the Warlike Genius
of Great Britain,'" writes Boswell, "came next in review.
The bard was a lank, bony figure, with short black hair.
He was writhing himself in agitation, while Johnson read,
and, showing his teeth in a grin of earnestness, exclaimed
in broken sentences, and in a keen, sharp tone : ' Is that
poetry, sir ?—is it Pindar ?' *Johnson :* 'Why, sir, there
is a great deal of what is called poetry !' Then, turning
to me, the poet cried : ' My muse has not been long upon
the town,' and pointing to the ode, ' it trembles under
the hand of the great critic !'"

The elder Disraeli told Mr. Croker that he was visited
by a Mr. Tasker, many years afterwards, at a watering-
place on the coast of Devon, and was so struck by his
resemblance to Boswell's description, that he asked the
gentleman if he had ever seen Dr. Johnson ; and the
visitor was, as he thought, the author of " The Ode to
the Warlike Genius of Great Britain."

In January, 1779, "The Club" suffered a great loss
by the death of Garrick, and Johnson insisted that there
should be a year's widowhood before a new member was
elected. "I saw old Samuel Johnson," writes Richard
Cumberland, "standing beside his (Garrick's) grave, at
the foot of Shakespeare's monument, and bathed in tears."
Topham Beauclerk, another intimate friend, died in March
of the following year, and Johnson felt his loss acutely.
" Poor dear Beauclerk," he writes to Boswell on the
8th of April, 1780—" 'nec ut soles, dabis joca '—his wit
and his folly, his acuteness and maliciousness, are now

over. Such another will not often be found among mankind." And he spoke of his death as "a loss that perhaps the whole nation could not repair."

In 1781, Johnson's friend, Mr. Thrale, who had for some time been very ill, died from a stroke of apoplexy. Everything of late had been left to the management of his wife, who looked after the business at Southwark, superintended the household affairs, and was untiring in her attentions to her husband. They were at this time staying in Grosvenor Square, where a house had been taken for the winter, to keep Mr. Thrale away from the worry of business. On the evening of the 3rd of April, his daughter Hester, better known as "Queenie" (afterwards Viscountess Keith), went down to her father's room and found him in a fit. From the first there was no hope, and the doctor thought it unnecessary even to prescribe. Johnson was sent for, and never left his friend's side till all was over. "I felt," he writes in his "Prayers and Meditations," "almost the last flutter of his pulse, and looked for the last time upon the face that for fifteen years had never been turned upon me but with respect or benignity."

The death of Mr. Thrale was, as might be expected, to make a great change in Johnson's relations with the family, but at present things went on as usual. He had been appointed one of the executors, and some amusement was caused by the business-like airs which he assumed for the occasion.

Boswell was now again in London, and relates a comical incident, which occurred after a dinner at Bolt Court, on Easter Sunday, where there were present, besides the writer himself, blind Mrs. Williams, Mrs. Desmoulins, Levett, Mrs. Hall (a sister of John Wesley, and very like him in figure and manner), and one or two others. Johnson made some remark, which both Mrs. Williams and Mrs. Hall tried to answer at the same time. The host was angry, and cried out, " Nay, when you both speak together it is intolerable ;" but, thinking he had been too harsh, added, " This one may say though, you are ladies ;" and, brightening into gay humour, quoted the lines from " The Beggar's Opera "—

" But two at a time there's no mortal can bear."

Boswell asked if he were going to turn Captain Macheath. " The contrast," he writes, " between Macheath, Polly, and Lucy—and Dr. Samuel Johnson, blind, peevish Mrs. Williams, and lean, lank, preaching Mrs. Hall, was exquisite."

A few days later Johnson had a pleasant dinner at Mrs. Garrick's, who still kept on the house in the Adelphi, and on this occasion, for the first time since her husband's death, received a few intimate friends. Among the company was the celebrated Miss Hannah More, who was more enthusiastic about Johnson than even Boswell. She had been introduced to him in 1773 or 1774, at Sir Joshua Reynolds' house, and Miss Reynolds soon afterwards took her to Bolt Court, where she was delighted with her reception. On another occasion Hannah More had the pleasure of receiving Johnson at a party at her own house, and after most of the company had retired, he and Garrick began a close encounter, telling old stories, " e'en from their boyish days " at

Lichfield. The conference was only broken up by the noise of a vociferous watchman, which warned them of the lateness of the hour.

The other guests at Mrs. Garrick's were Johnson himself, Mrs. Elizabeth Carter, his former collaborator in *The Gentleman's Magazine,* Boswell, Mrs. Boscawen—"the high-bred, elegant Boscawen" of the Streatham verses—Sir Joshua Reynolds, and Dr. Burney, the father of Fanny Burney. The entertainment went off very agreeably, and as Johnson and Boswell walked home together, they stopped on the Adelphi Terrace, overlooking the river, and talked of the two friends they had lost, Beauclerk and Garrick; "two such friends," said Johnson, tenderly, "as cannot be supplied." Mrs. Garrick survived this evening more than forty-one years, and was buried in her wedding sheets in her husband's grave, in the Abbey, on the 25th of October, 1822. There is an interesting description of her, quoted in Dean Stanley's "Memorials of Westminster Abbey," as "a little, broken-down old woman, who went about leaning on a gold-headed cane, dressed in deep widow's mourning, and always talking of her dear 'Davy.'"

In the autumn Johnson was absent from London some months, and paid visits to Oxford, Lichfield, Birmingham, and Ashbourne. "Dear Dr. Johnson is at length returned," writes Mrs. Thrale, on the 17th of December; "he has been a vast while away, to see his country folks at Lichfield."

Early in 1782 Robert Levett, his old and faithful friend, died very suddenly. This curious character had, in his youth, picked up some knowledge of medicine in

Paris, and, on his return to London, took lodgings at the house of an attorney, in Northumberland Court, and set up as a physician.   He had long been an inmate of Johnson's establishment, and his particular part in the routine of the household was to pour out the tea for his host at breakfast, of which meal he always had a share. He had an extensive practice, but among the very poorest class.   Johnson had a high opinion of his skill, and liked his companionship.   His death made a gap among Johnson's friends, which he often alluded to with regret.

During this year, his intercourse with Mrs. Thrale was still kept up, and there was no outward cessation of friendship, but it was evident that it could not be continued on its former footing.   Mrs. Thrale herself confessed that, without her husband's assistance, she did not feel herself able to entertain Johnson as a constant inmate of her house.   In the beginning of 1782, she spent three months in London, but returned to Streatham in April. Miss Burney had already discovered her friend's tender feelings for Piozzi, but they appear, at that time, not to have been remarked by Johnson.   In September, the place at Streatham was, from motives of economy, let to Lord Shelburne, and Mrs. Thrale took a house at Brighton, whither Johnson accompanied her, and remained six weeks on the old familiar footing.   On this point the diary of Madame d'Arblay, who was, at that time, a guest of Mrs. Thrale's, bears unimpeachable evidence.   It is strange that of this visit to Brighton Boswell makes no mention.

The real facts of the case appear to be that Mrs. Thrale was unwilling to break off her connection with

Johnson, of which she was extremely proud, but wished his visits to be less frequent, and he either did not, or would not, understand her. At present, however, there was nothing like an open rupture.

In March, 1783, Boswell came to town, and was glad to find Johnson at Mrs. Thrale's house in Argyle Street, appearances of friendship being still kept up, but Boswell thought him very ill, as he undoubtedly was. Asthmatic symptoms had shown themselves, and he looked "pale and distressed." Hannah More, too, about the same time, writes: "Poor Johnson is in a bad state of health; I fear his constitution is breaking up." But he rallied somewhat in the summer, and was well enough to be a most effective cicerone to Hannah More during her visit to Oxford. He showed her over his old college, and pointed out the rooms of his former comrades, and when they came to the common room they found a large print of Johnson, framed, and hung up, that very day, with a motto below it from Miss More's "Sensibility :"

> "And is not Johnson ours? himself a host."

The gloomy apprehensions of his friends for Johnson's health were too well founded. Early in the morning of the 17th of June, shortly after his visit to Oxford, he had a severe paralytic stroke, which deprived him of speech. But he retained the full use of his senses, and was able to write a few lines on a card to beg his neighbour, Mr. Edmund Allen, the printer, to come and act for him "as the emergencies of the case might require." He sent another letter to his schoolfellow, Dr. Taylor, asking to see him as soon as possible, and requesting that he would bring with him Dr. Heberden, who, at that time, was, almost, without a rival in his profession. Two days later, he wrote a long account of his seizure to Mrs. Thrale, then settled at Bath with her daughters. On receipt of the bad news, she wished to come to London, at once, to look after him. "Your offer, dear madam, of coming to me," he wrote in reply, "is charmingly kind; but I will lay it up for future use;" and he finished his letter "write to me very often."

Owing to his robust constitution, Johnson's health was soon partially restored. He was able, early in July, to dine at the "Club," and soon after to pay some visits in the country; but life had lost a good deal of its zest, and there was much to sadden him at home. On the 5th of July, he writes to his step-daughter, Lucy Porter: "I live now but in a melancholy way; my old friend, Mr. Levett, is dead, who lived with me in the house, and was useful and companionable; Mrs. Desmoulins is gone away; and Mrs. Williams is so much decayed that she can add little to another's gratifications." Mrs. Desmoulins soon returned to Bolt Court, and helped to nurse Johnson in his last illness, but Mrs. Williams died in September.

In this autumn, 1783, Johnson received a visit at his house from Mrs. Siddons, the greatest actress of the English stage. Her brother, Charles Kemble, equally celebrated in the same profession, left a pleasant account of his sister's reception at Bolt Court. "When Mrs. Siddons came into the room," he writes, "there happened to be no chair ready for her, which he observing said, with a smile, 'You, madam, who so often occasion a want of seats to other people, will the more easily excuse the want of one yourself.' Having placed himself by her, he, with great good humour, entered upon a consideration of the English drama; and, among other inquiries, particularly asked her which of Shakespeare's characters she was most pleased with. Upon her answering that she thought the character of Queen Catherine, in Henry the Eighth, the most natural; 'I think so, too, madam,' said he, 'and whenever you perform it, I will once more hobble out to the theatre.' Mrs. Siddons said she would do herself the honour of acting his favourite part for him; but she had no opportunity of fulfilling her promise before the doctor's death."

In the winter, the survivors of the old " Ivy Lane Club " dined together twice, at the Queen's Arms in St. Paul's Churchyard, and later on were entertained at Johnson's house. At his suggestion, another club was instituted, which met at the Essex Head Tavern, in Essex Street, kept by an old servant of Mrs. Thrale's. It was continued for some years, and was still flourishing in 1792.

Boswell was very anxious, this year, for Johnson to accept Mr. Wilkes's hospitality, and that gentleman, who had now retired from political life, and held a lucrative municipal office, sent the doctor an invitation to dinner. He was unfortunately engaged, and the entertainment never came off. Johnson's reply to Mr. and Miss Wilkes's invitation is preserved among the MSS. of the British Museum.

In the beginning of 1784, Johnson's health appeared

somewhat improved, and Boswell, on arriving in London, found him in better spirits than he had been for some time. On the 5th of June, they made an excursion to Oxford, where they spent nearly a fortnight as guests of Johnson's fellow collegian, Dr. Adams, then master of Pembroke College. On his return to London, though he looked and felt far from well, he was constantly dining out, and in no way following the *régime* of an invalid. We hear of him at Mr. Dilly's, the bookseller, at General Paoli's, and, more than once, at Reynolds's. On the 22nd he dined, for the last time, at the "Club," where he was much pleased with the kindness and deference that was shown him by every one.

It was either during this, or the previous year, that Mary Wollstonecraft, afterwards the mother of Mary Shelley, paid a visit to Johnson at Bolt Court. William Godwin, her husband, relates the circumstances as follows : " It was also during her residence at Newington Green that she was introduced to the acquaintance of Dr. Johnson, who was at that time considered, as in some sort, the father of English literature. The doctor treated her with particular kindness and attention, had a long conversation with her, and desired her to repeat her visit often. This she firmly purposed to do, but the news of his last illness, and then of his death, intervened to prevent her seeing him a second time."

This interview has a strong suggestive interest. Mary Wollstonecraft's character was in her own time misunderstood and misrepresented ; and she was throughout life unfortunate in her surroundings. Her father was a cruel tyrant in his own family, and after her mother's death, Mary, then a young and beautiful woman, determined to support herself by her own exertions. When she made the acquaintance of Johnson, she was keeping a school, which was doing well, and promised to be a success, but on hearing of the illness of a young married lady, to whom she was tenderly attached, she left the place, where she was enjoying happiness and independence, to watch by the death-bed of her friend. When the sad event was over, she engaged for a time in literary work, and, a few years later, made the acquaintance of a Mr. Imlay, in whose honour she allowed herself to confide. This worthless scoundrel entrapped her into some kind of marriage at Paris, and basely deserted her, after she had borne him a child, and had injured her health by her exertions to retrieve his ruined fortunes. Her second husband, William Godwin, was a dull pedant, as intolerant in his political opinions as in his religious scepticism. Mary Wollstonecraft was foolish enough to despise public opinion, and she hated the bigotry and the religious intolerance of those formal times, but no more noble-minded woman ever lived. Her worst enemies have never dared to say that she had erred from profligate motives, or that she had lost the innate purity of her mind. From her earliest youth, her life was spent in trying to help those who were unhappy or unfortunate, and though she differed from Johnson in every outward circumstance of her life and opinions, there was one strong point of resemblance—a great love of humanity.

It is not the duty of a biographer to indulge in hypothetical speculations, but it is well to consider what a

different career might have been that of Mary Wollstonecraft, if the course of events had allowed this visit at
Bolt Court to be repeated, and the acquaintance, which
had given so much pleasure to both, to develop into friendship and intimacy.

Johnson's state of health had now become so bad
that efforts were made by his friends to procure some
increase to his pension, which would enable him to travel
on the Continent, and try the effects of a milder climate.
But the project was unsuccessful, though Lord Thurlow,
then Lord Chancellor, had promised to exert his influence
in the affair, and even offered himself to advance £500
on the formal security of the pension. Liberal offers of
pecuniary assistance were made by private friends, but
Dr. Brocklesby, Johnson's regular attendant, thought that
little advantage would be gained by a foreign residence,
and the scheme was abandoned. Boswell was now
obliged to return to Scotland, and on the 30th of June,
after a dinner at Sir Joshua Reynolds's, he drove with
Johnson to the entrance of Bolt Court, and took an
affectionate farewell. It was the last time they were to
meet, and Boswell had evidently some forebodings of the
loss he was soon to undergo. He had many kind ac-
quaintances, who were attracted by his geniality and good
nature, but of the literary circle, with which he associated, there were none except Johnson, and Reynolds,
who entertained for him any serious feelings of regard.
Reynolds, undoubtedly, had a great liking for him, which
was always retained, and he was one of those mentioned
in the great painter's will, but Johnson's feelings towards him were still warmer. He had declared that to

lose Boswell would be like the amputation of a limb, and, notwithstanding the occasional rebukes which he administered, there was no person whose society always gave him so much satisfaction. It would have been well for Boswell, if he had been able to form other friendships of the same nature.

On the 30th of June, Mrs. Thrale announced to Johnson her intended marriage, which did not, however, take place till the 25th of July. The news can hardly have been a surprise to him, if the account is correct, which Madame d'Arblay gives in her Diary of her interview with Johnson, in the November of the preceding year. He replied in an angry tone, under the belief that the marriage had already taken place. In any case, however, no practical result could have arisen from the correspondence, which ended with a letter from Mrs. Thrale, bidding him a " kind and affectionate farewell." But his wrath was not to be appeased, and he never spoke of her again except in language of the strongest contempt and indignation. The whole dispute seems, in the present day, entirely uncalled for, but the marriage offended some of Johnson's strongest prejudices. He hated a fiddler, and he hated a foreigner, and Piozzi was both ; and in his unreasoning anger he could write in no gentler terms to the woman whom he had so long "loved, esteemed, and reverenced," than to tell her, " If you have abandoned your children and your religion, God forgive your wickedness ; if you have forfeited your fame and your country, may your folly do you no further mischief." Johnson was without doubt sincere in the conviction that he was acting rightly, and the step which Mrs. Thrale was taking, appeared in his

eyes an unpardonable offence. "Poor Thrale," he wrote
to Hawkins, "I thought that either her virtue or her vice
[meaning by the former the love of her children and by
the latter her pride] would have kept her from such a
marriage." It was impossible that the close friendship
could have been continued as formerly, but those, who
love and honour Johnson's memory, must regret the
manner in which the separation took place.

Johnson was now quite aware of the gravity of his
illness, and he knew that the end could not be far off.
He was evidently desirous of arranging his affairs, and
one of his anxieties was to place some memorial to his
wife in the church at Bromley, where she was buried.
He wrote to the clergyman of the parish and requested
permission to lay a stone over her grave, and the design
was carried out. It is a plain recumbent slab, near the
middle of the centre aisle, and the inscription composed
by himself is (or was a few years ago) still quite legible.
On the 13th of July, he left London and spent some weeks
at Ashbourne. From there he went to Lichfield, and
his native air gave him some temporary relief. "My
dropsy is gone," he writes on September 29th, "and my
asthma is remitted, but I have felt myself a little declining these two days, or, at least, to-day." The decline,
alas, was to go on very rapidly.

At Lichfield there was a gravestone erected to the
memory of Elizabeth Blaney, by Johnson's father, whom
the girl had probabl known in his "prentice days,"
at Leeke, and followed to Lichfield, where she died.
Johnson had this romantic memorial of his father's
early history repaired and restored, but it has now,

unfortunately, disappeared. He also ordered a large stone to be laid over his parents grave in St. Michael's church, and composed an epitaph for it. This interesting relic was lost when the floor was repaired in 1796, and quite recently some Staffordshire worthies have placed a slab, with a copy of the old inscription, in the same church.

Johnson never lost his affection for his native place. "Its inhabitants," he said, "were more orthodox in their religion, more pure in their language, and more polite in their manners than any other town in the kingdom." The purity of their language, or, at all events, of their pronunciation, is rather questionable. Johnson to the last retained some of his provincial accents ; and Boswell tells us that "Garrick used to take him off squeezing a lemon into a punch-bowl with uncouth gesticulations, looking round the company and calling out 'Who's for poonsh?'" Garrick himself, however, was not quite faultless in this respect ; and, according to Dr. Burney, he always said, "*shupreme,*" "*shuperior.*"

There is an interesting trace of Johnson's last visit to Lichfield in the library of the cathedral. His name appears in the lending book as having borrowed Sir John Floyer's work on the asthma, in the hope, no doubt, of finding some instructions which might afford relief to his own case. In a letter to Langton, written at this time, he says: "nor does it [the asthma] lay very close siege to life, for Sir John Floyer, whom the physical race consider as author of one of the best books upon it, panted on till ninety." The little volume is still carefully preserved in the cathedral library. Sir John Floyer, him-

self a Lichfield man, and a physician of some note, was
the author of several scientific works, some of which were
published by Michael Johnson.

From Lichfield, Johnson went on to Birmingham, to pass
a short time with his old schoolfellow Hector, who wrote
to Boswell that their chief delight had been in recalling
the events of early days.   On his way home, he stopped
a short time at Oxford, where he was again the guest of
Dr. Adams, and he finally returned to Bolt Court on
November 17th.   While he was away he had kept up an
active correspondence with his friends, and there are
letters from him to Dr. Burney, Hoole, Bennet Langton,
Windham, Reynolds, and Tom Davies the bookseller.
During his absence, Edmund Allen, his intimate friend,
and neighbour at Bolt Court, had died, and Johnson
wrote to John Nichols, the antiquary : " I hope we shall be
much together.   You must now be to me what you were
before, and what dear Mr. Allen was besides."

Boswell was all this time "silent and sullen." He had
been foolish enough to take offence at a very sensible
admonition that Johnson had written to him in the previous July, advising him to write " like a man," and " to
leave off affecting discontent, and indulging the vanity of
complaint."   Two days after this letter was sent, Johnson,
with great kindness, wrote again, begging it might not be
taken amiss, but, for more than three months, he waited
in vain for a reply.   Boswell's childish vanity was
wounded by a few words of merited reproof from his
" *revered* friend," now in his 76th year, and who was fast
sinking into the grave.

By the time Johnson arrived in London, both the

dropsy and asthma had made rapid progress, and his nights were sleepless and without rest. Nothing, however, could exceed the kindness of his friends, who were unremitting in their attentions. Fanny Burney paid, what was to be, her farewell visit on November 25th, and had a long conversation with him alone. She called a second time, but he was too ill to receive her. Bennet Langton took a room in Fleet Street, close by, and tended him with almost filial affection. Windham, then at the outset of his distinguished career, forgot for a time the cares and excitement of party to watch by the side of his dying friend. "God bless you, dear Windham," said Johnson, the day before his death, and added a wish that they "might share some humble portion of that happiness which God vouchsafes to repentant sinners." It was the last time that Windham ever heard the sound of his voice. Edmund Burke too was sometimes there, and on one occasion expressed his fears that Johnson might find the numbers oppressive. "No, sir," he said, "it is not so, and I must be in a wretched state indeed when your company would not be a delight to me." Dr. Heberden and Dr. Brocklesby were in constant attendance, and did everything that unwearied patience and great skill could suggest to alleviate his sufferings, but refused to receive any reward for their services.

At the end of November, he made his will, and arranged for the payment of some trifling debts. He wrote an affectionate letter to his step-daughter, Lucy Porter, and asked for her prayers. Nothing was left for him now but to prepare to die. Though a stranger to fear, in the presence of mere bodily danger, he had

never concealed his dread at the thoughts of death. He
was, formerly, often heard to mutter to himself the lines
from Shakespeare—

> "Ay, but to die, and go we know not where ;
> To lie in cold obstruction and to rot ;
> This sensible warm motion to become
> A kneaded clod." [1]

"No rational man," he once said, "could die without
uneasy apprehension." But when his last hour came,
all feelings of alarm and mistrust had disappeared, and
he expressed his perfect faith in the merits and propitia-
tion of his Redeemer. His intellect was perfectly clear
to the last, and only a few days before his death, when the
doctors disapproved of some remedy, which he had tried
without their sanction, he repeated Swift's lines, from the
"Verses on the Death of Doctor Swift."

> "The doctors, tender of their fame,
> Wisely on him lay all the blame ;
> We must confess his case was nice ;
> But he could never take advice.
> Had he been rul'd, for aught appears,
> He might have liv'd these twenty years."

Mr. Windham's servant, who sat up with him during
his last night, declared that "no man could appear more
collected, more devout, or less terrified at the thoughts
of the approaching minute." At the interval of each
hour, they assisted him to sit up in bed, and move his
legs, which were in much pain, and he urgently addressed
himself to fervent prayer. In the morning, he was still

[1] "Measure for Measure," act ii. scene 1.

able to give his blessing to Miss Morris, the sister of the beautiful girl, who sat to Reynolds for the well-known picture of Hope nursing Love. When she came into the room, he turned himself in his bed, and said, "God bless you, my dear." They were the last words he ever spoke. In the afternoon he became drowsy, and when the doctors came for their usual visit, he was in a kind of doze, and spoke to no one. In the evening, at about a quarter past seven, he passed away without pain or uneasiness on the 13th of December, 1784, in his 76th year. His last moments were so peaceful that Mrs. Desmoulins and Francis Barber, who were in the same room, scarcely knew the exact hour of his death.

He was buried on Monday, December 20th, in Westminster Abbey, almost at the foot of the Shakespeare monument, and close to the remains of his old pupil, David Garrick. The service was performed by his schoolfellow, Dr. Taylor, and, among the pall-bearers, were Burke, Windham, and Bennet Langton. Over his grave, according to his request, was placed a plain stone, with this inscription,

SAMUEL JOHNSON, LL.D.,
Obiit xiii. die Decembris
Anno Domini
M,DCC.LXXXIV.
Ætatis suæ LXXV.

CHAPTER IX.

JOHNSON'S character, though it contained many contradictions, is not difficult to understand. Its salient points were manliness, generosity, high courage, humanity, and a strict adherence to truth. He was singularly straightforward and upright in every action of his life. He hated meanness, and had a profound contempt for the *suspicions* of busybodies, who occupied themselves in watching their neighbour's affairs. "Those who look on the ground," he once said, "cannot avoid seeing dirt." His fervid piety was undoubted, but he was not entirely free from superstition. His belief in spirits and apparitions, however, has been greatly exaggerated. He thought that the universal traditions of supernatural agencies, which have prevailed in all ages, were an interesting subject of inquiry; and he argued that a total denial of their possibility would imply an opinion, adverse to the existence of the soul between death and the last day. From his profound veneration for the Church of England, he was intolerant of dissent, which appeared to him a sign of presumption and folly; but in discussing religion, as an abstract question, he, sometimes, expressed opinions which would almost be thought latitudinarian, even in our own day. "For my part, sir," he declared to Boswell, "I think all Christians, whether Papists or Protestants, agree in the essential articles, and that their differences are trivial, and rather political than religious." His horror of infidelity was extreme. He would not suffer in his presence any controversy as to the truth of revealed religion, and this seemed partly to proceed from a strange dread lest his own faith might be shaken.

For mere sentimental suffering he had little sympathy, and, sometimes, he expressed his opinions on the subject rather harshly. His own strong constitution made him unable to understand the bodily weaknesses of others who were less robust. "Why do you shiver, sir?" he said to Boswell, as they were returning home from Greenwich by the river on a cold evening. And at another time, he was indignant with his companion in a post-chaise who complained of headache. "When I was your age, sir," he declared angrily, "I had no headaches." But for real suffering, his compassion was unbounded, and he could never see a case of distress without wishing to relieve it. He was in the habit of keeping loose money in his pocket to give to the starving creatures whom he met in his walks. When staying at Lichfield, he used to confide to Lucy Porter a sufficient sum to pay his return journey to London, so certain was he to give away every farthing he had in his own possession. To Mrs. Desmoulins, one of his pensioners in Bolt Court, he allowed a weekly sum of 10s., when his whole income was only £300 a year; and in his early days, while still wretchedly poor, he was constantly endeavouring to help those who were poorer than himself. This genuine feeling of charity was constant throughout life. He once administered a severe rebuke to Mrs. Thrale, who, after a very hot summer of drought, complained peevishly of the dust on the Surrey roads. "I cannot bear," he said with an altered look, "when I know how many poor families will perish next winter, for want of that bread which the present drought will deny them, to hear ladies sighing for rain, only that their complexions may not suffer from the heat, or their clothes be incommoded by the dust." He would have been delighted with the reproof which Lord Rutherford received from a Highland shepherd, near Bonaly among the Pentlands. The story is told by Dean Ramsay, in his "Reminiscences." His lordship was complaining of the weather, which prevented him enjoying his visit to the country, and said in a moment of unguarded haste, "What a d———d mist." The shepherd, a tall grim figure, turned sharply round on him, "What ails ye at the mist, sir? It weets the sod, it slockens the yowes, and," with much solemnity, "it's God's will."

His personal courage was undoubted, and neither Foote nor Macpherson cared to put it to a practical test. Garrick told Mrs. Thrale of an anecdote of Johnson at the Lichfield theatre. He had placed a chair for himself on the stage, but during his momentary absence, it was taken. On his return he requested the intruder to move, and on his refusal flung both the chair and its occupier into the pit. "This story," Johnson said, when questioned on the subject, "was very nearly true." In his French tour, when he was driving in a carriage with the Thrales, between Vernon and St. Denis, the horses ran away on the brink of a precipice, and the escape of the party was almost miraculous. But he refused to believe there had been any real danger, for "nothing came out of it," he said, "except that Thrale leapt out of the carriage into a chalk pit, and came back looking as if he had seen a ghost, and almost as white."

His colloquial powers were extraordinary. His command of language, his readiness, his richness of illustration and vast erudition made him undoubtedly one of the best conversationalists of his time ; and it required not only boldness, but a great deal of self-command, to contest with him. Few indeed, except Burke and Reynolds, ever made the attempt. One of his favourite methods of argument was a flat denial of his opponent's statements, and he considered that treating an adversary with respect was giving him an advantage to which he was not entitled. His step-daughter, Lucy Porter, once said to a clergyman, who had offended her, "Why you are just like Dr. Johnson, you contradict every word one speaks."

His incredulity was almost beyond belief. Hogarth said he was like King David, for "he said in his haste all men are liars." Two gentlemen who were dining at Streatham, in 1782, were talking of Elliot's defence of Gibraltar, and one of them mentioned the red-hot cannon balls, which had been used on that occasion. After listening for a time, Johnson said, with a cold sneer, "I would advise you, sir, never to relate this story again ; you really can scarce imagine how *very poor* a figure you make in the telling of it." When Mrs. Thrale remonstrated with him afterwards, he answered, "Why, madam, if a creature is neither capable

of giving dignity to falsehood, nor willing to remain con-
tented with the truth, he deserves no better treatment."
He seemed, however, to be quite unaware of his own
rudeness.   He said, with perfect gravity to Boswell, " I
consider myself a very polite man;" and, at another time,
he remarked to Mrs. Thrale, in speaking of Dr. Barnard,
Provost of Eton, "He was the only man, too, that did
justice to my good breeding, and you may observe that
I am well-bred to a degree of needless scrupulosity.
No man," he continued, not observing the amazement
of his hearers, "is so cautious not to interrupt another;
no man thinks it so necessary to appear attentive when
others are speaking ; no man so steadily refuses pre-
ference to himself, or so readily bestows it on another,
as I do ; nobody holds so strongly, as I do, the necessity of
ceremony, and the ill effects which follow the breach
of it; yet people think me rude, but Barnard did me
justice."

Johnson has never been highly estimated as a critic,
and on this point he has hardly received fair consideration.
His hasty remarks, uttered in the heat of controversy,
have been handed down as the result of deliberate
judgment, but his literary instincts were more correct
than has generally been imagined.   Personal feelings
undoubtedly often influenced his opinions, and he was
unwilling to allow praise to writers of whose principles he
disapproved.   He could see little merit in the vigorous
irony of Swift, and would never acknowledge him to be
the author of "The Tale of a Tub!" but there is
scarcely any writer from whom Johnson quoted so
often in his dictionary.   "Swift," he said, "was in

coarse humour inferior to Arbuthnot, and in refined humour inferior to Addison." Arbuthnot, indeed, he thought to be first man of his time. He called Fielding a "blockhead" and a "barren rascal," but he confessed to having read through "Amelia" without stopping, and thought the heroine one of the most pleasing characters in fiction. For the delightful mixture of wit and pathos in the description of "Uncle Toby" he had no appreciation, and said that "Tristram Shandy" would soon be forgotten. But when Goldsmith asserted that Sterne was a dull fellow, he would not agree, and, without further comment, blurted out, "Why, no, sir."

On the other hand, he spoke too favourably of writers whose personal characters he respected. Beattie he loved, and he mentioned his writings in terms which now appear ludicrous. He was under obligations to Richardson, and thought highly of the moral tendency of his works, which in consequence he immensely over-rated, but he admitted that anybody who read Richardson's novels for the sake of the story would be compelled to hang himself, and forgot the fact that it is exactly *for the sake of the story* that novels are generally read, and that, however excellent may be the sentiment, the reader of a work of fiction will soon close the volume if there is no amusement in the plot. It would be interesting to learn what Johnson thought of the broad humour of "Peregrine Pickle," but he is not known to have expressed any opinion on Smollett as a writer, though they must, in some manner, have been acquainted. It was partly through Smollett's exertions that Frank Barber got his discharge, when he was pressed on board the *Stag* frigate, in 1759, and in after days Johnson repaid the service by correcting the epitaph, composed for Smollett's monument, on the banks of the Leven.   Johnson had a keen appre-ciation of Bunyan and Cervantes, and he thought " Don Quixote " the greatest work in the world after Homer's " Iliad."

His opinions of the poets are well known from his "Lives," which have been already alluded to.   It is difficult to understand how he can have preferred Akenside to Gray, but the works of the latter never appealed to his feelings.   They wanted earnestness and pathos to suit his taste, and he was not fascinated by the exquisite beauty of their language.   No one probably will blame him for his poor opinion of Mason and Collins; but he rather unjustly depreciated Churchill, whose satire is often powerful and amusing.   He allowed the excellence of Young, and declared that the " Night Thoughts " was one of " the few poems in which blank verse could not be changed for rhyme but with disadvan-tage."   Thomson's poetry appeared to him to contain a real vein of genius, and he gave high praise to " The Seasons." " The Traveller," he asserted, was the finest poem that had appeared since the days of Pope, and " The Deserted Village " he thought almost as good, though perhaps too much an echo of it.   For Pope and Dryden he had the greatest admiration.   The former he considered the more uniformly excellent, though the latter had finer passages than any written by Pope.   Prior was not one of his favourite authors, but he was right in saying that the poet wrote of love like a man who had never

felt it. The earlier poets were seldom alluded to in his
conversation. Chaucer's "Canterbury Tales" he may
have liked; but he could have had little sympathy for
the dreamland in which Spenser appeared to live. The
good damsel Una, the false Duessa, the knights, and the
dragons of "The Fairy Queen" must have appeared to
him unreal, and he could hardly have been one of the
select few who, in the language of Macaulay, "were in
at the death of the beast."

To the genius of Shakespeare he rendered due homage,
and he was well acquainted with his plays, but he was not
enthusiastic on the subject. Like the schoolboy who
dislikes Horace, he had probably unpleasant recollections
of his protracted and uncongenial labours in preparing
his edition of the great poet. He appeared to have given
little attention to the dramatists of the Restoration period.
"The Rehearsal" had not, in his judgment, "wit enough
to preserve its vitality," and Bayes he thought a silly part
and not intended for Dryden. Of the later writers for
the stage, he admired Farquhar, though he hardly did
full justice to the brilliant author of "The Beaux
Stratagem" and "The Recruiting Officer." Of contemporary comedies, he thought that Goldsmith's "Good-
natured Man" was the best that had appeared since
"The Provoked Husband." He had too high an
opinion of Murphy's plays, now almost forgotten, but
his judgment in this case was no doubt influenced by
personal feelings. "The Rivals" and "The Trip to
Scarborough" ("The School for Scandal" had not then
appeared) by Richard Brinsley Sheridan, were, he declared,
the two best comedies of the age, and this opinion has

been emphatically endorsed by the immense popularity which they have retained to the present day.

He thought the first part of Burnet's "History of his Own Time" one of the most entertaining books of the language. Robertson's "Histories" were, in his opinion, mere verbiage, and he confessed that he had never read Hume. Goldsmith's "Histories" he considered to be extremely useful. "Goldsmith," he said, "tells you shortly all you want to know; and his plain narrative will please again and again." He disliked Gibbon's principles too heartily to pronounce an impartial opinion on his writings, but his famous work, "The Decline and Fall of the Roman Empire," was only completed shortly before Johnson's death. Of English divines he thought that Atterbury, South, Seed, Jortin, Sherlock, and Smalridge were in the first rank. Tillotson was a dangerous writer, he said, to imitate; but he praised Blair's sermons, though the author was a Scotchman and a Presbyterian. In any consideration of Johnson's views on theology, we must bear in mind the period in which he lived. The religious feeling of the country in those days was almost as cold and inanimate as among the Buddhists of modern China. The only hope of salvation was considered to be in a dull and formal orthodoxy. The preaching of Whitefield and the Wesleys had hardly begun to rouse the Church of England from its long slumber. Among the lower ranks of the clergy, it is scarcely possible to mention more than one or two names of any eminence, either in literature or in their own profession. No one has ever suggested that the description of Parson Trulliber was much exaggerated; and Parson Adams, in "Joseph

Andrews," and Dr. Primrose, in "The Vicar of Wakefield," were certainly intended as very favourable specimens
of their class. The London pulpits were occupied by
preachers of so little learning or eloquence that their
congregations must have watched with intense anxiety the
sand running down the hour-glass in front of the pulpit.
It is difficult to recall the name of any incumbent of a
metropolitan parish, whose sermons are now remembered,
and the bishops, with a few exceptions, were not much
more distinguished than the inferior clergy. There was
Warburton, Bishop of Gloucester, who commenced life as
an attorney, and had afterwards taken orders, as Churchill
pretended—

> "thereto drawn,
> By some faint omens of the lawn."

He had been raised to the bench for his edition of
Pope's Works, and had obtained a kind of reflected
glory from his intimacy with the poet. His reading was
undoubtedly extensive, but a good deal of his time must
have been occupied in his protracted controversy with
his right reverend brother, Lowth, Bishop of London.
The dispute was alluded to by George III. in his famous
conversation with Johnson, and the sovereign seemed to
think that the argument was pretty well at an end, when
the two prelates had taken to call one another names.
But Bishop Lowth was a man of much greater moral
weight and sounder learning than Warburton, and his
Commentary on Isaiah is still a standard work. Joseph
Butler, Bishop of Durham, was one of the most profound
thinkers of his time. His "Analogy" is to this day
used as a text-book on Divinity, and is probably the best

work of the sort on the subject. There were other
eminent prelates such as Bishop Newton, who wrote on
prophecy, Bishop Horsley, Bishop Hurd, and Bishop
Pearce, but they are now little known.

If during this period · the religious annals of the
country were devoid of interest, its literary history was
still more barren, and nothing, like a love of choice
books or rare editions, seems to have been known.
Garrick was supposed to have many valuable volumes of
the early dramatists, and especially of Shakespeare, but
his interest in the subject was professional.   It is curious
to examine the catalogue of the library, formed by
Topham Beauclerk, a man of culture, of refined taste,
and the possessor of a good income.   In his vast collection, there appears none of the first four folios of
Shakespeare, nor any of the original quartos.   There was
no copy of the first edition of Spenser's " Fairy Queen,"
no old black letter Chaucer, and not a single volume,
printed by Caxton, or Wynkyn de Worde.   Among the
foreign books, there were no valuable copies of "Rabelais,"
nor a single specimen of any first edition of Molière ; and
the earliest " Don Quixote," in the collection, was of
1738.   Among classics, which, in those times, formed
such an important part of a gentleman's library, there
was one " Editio Princeps," an Aldine copy of Aristo-
phanes, which at the auction, after Beauclerk's death, was
sold for the princely sum of £1 7s.   The sale lasted fifty
days, and the entire sum realized was little more than, in
recent times, has been paid at Sotheby's for a single
volume.   The only English work, which fetched anything
like an exceptional price, was a complete set of the original

Spectators, which were sold for £12, about six times its present value.

Johnson lived between two brilliant epochs of literature. When he first arrived in London in 1737, few of the eminent writers of our Augustan era still remained. Addison, Prior, Steele, Arbuthnot, and John Gay were dead. Swift, fast sinking into a "driveller and a show,"[1] had left England never to return, and was an exile in the country for which he did so much, and which he never ceased to hate and despise. Pope was still at Twickenham, dragging on his sickly life, and in the ensuing year brought out the last of his Satires, at the same time as the appearance of Johnson's "London." Not long afterwards Reynolds saw him for the first and only time, and in later days described to Malone the personal appearance of the poet. The incident occurred at a crowded auction of pictures, and a whisper went through the room, "Mr. Pope! Mr. Pope!" A passage was made for him as he passed, and Reynolds, through the arm of some one standing before him, managed to touch the poet's hand. He was "about four feet six inches high; very hump-backed and deformed. He wore a black coat, and according to the fashion of that time, had on a little sword. He had a large and fine eye, and a long, handsome nose; his mouth had those peculiar marks which are always found in the mouths of crooked persons, and the muscles which run across the cheek were so strongly marked that they seemed like small cords." He survived till 1744.

Bolingbroke, the brilliant orator and statesman, and

[1] Johnson's "Vanity of Human Wishes."

unsurpassed as a political writer, was returned from his banishment in France, and had now abundant opportunities of enjoying that freedom from public cares, which he had formerly affected to desire. Though still consumed by restless ambition, he was no longer in a position to exercise any influence on affairs of State. His active career was finished, and before long he was to retire to the family Manor House at Battersea, and, a martyr to the most painful of all complaints, to end his life in solitude and neglect. Part of the old building is still standing, and contains one room of special interest. Pope, who was on most intimate terms with Bolingbroke, and a frequent guest under his roof, must have passed many hours in the cedar wainscotted parlour which looks upon the river.

On the death of Johnson, Wordsworth, the originator of a new school of poetry, and, it may almost be said, the founder of a new school of thought, was a boy of fourteen; Walter Scott, about twelve months younger than Wordsworth, was in a few years to record, both in prose and verse, the ballads and traditions of his country, and to arouse among its inhabitants feelings of national enthusiasm, greater than they had ever before known. Byron and Shelley were not yet born, but the time was not far distant, when they were to astonish the world by their genius and audacity. Keats, a few years younger than his two famous contemporaries, and in his own time the object of bitter irony and ridicule, was to publish two small volumes, which half a century later were to be frequently sold for about thirty times their original cost, and to obtain for the author a reputation beyond the highest dreams of his ambition.

Johnson, during the latter part of his career, occupied a position of remarkable eminence, and he was perhaps more known and written about than any man in the kingdom. Of the small circle, which then composed the literary world, he was the undoubted chief, and his authority was never questioned. It has been generally imagined that during his lifetime, his reputation was derived entirely from his writings, and that the colloquial fame on which his renown now chiefly rests, was the result of Boswell's "Life." This is hardly correct. Reynolds, in a short character of Johnson, which he drew up, probably for Boswell, writes, "It has been frequently observed that he was a singular instance of a man, who had so much distinguished himself by his writings, that his conversation not only supported his character as an author, but, in the opinion of many, was superior." There is indeed reason to believe that, with the exception of "Rasselas," and "The Lives of the Poets," his works, even in their own day, inspired a Platonic interest, and were, in fact, more talked of than read. The famous biography has undoubtedly given us many details of his manners and habits, of which his most intimate companions had never heard, but his great conversational powers were well known many years before his death, and his witty sayings and repartees were constantly recorded in the newspapers and magazines of the period. In 1776, a little volume was published under the title of "Johnsoniana, or Bon Mots of Dr. Johnson," which, he said, was "a mighty impudent thing," but it had a large sale. The collection contained many of his sayings, not told with anything approaching to the skill displayed by Boswell, but which all were, more or less, authentic, and most of them are indeed found in an improved form in Boswell's own book. There are many portraits of Johnson, but by far the finest is the head size by Reynolds, formerly in Sir Robert Peel's collection, and now in the National Gallery, of which there is a superb mezzotint engraving by Doughty. Johnson's personal appearance improved much in his later years. The scars on his face had softened down, his convulsive movements were less frequent, and his manner and tone were gentler. His features must always have been striking and impressive, and in relating an anecdote, or reciting poetry, his facial expression must have been skilful and effective. He generally wore a brown suit with twisted hair buttons of the same colour, a large bluish grey wig, a plain shirt, and black worsted stockings. The sleeves of his coat were loose, and he wore no ruffles, so that his white shirt sleeves were visible, as shown in the picture mentioned above. As he grew older he became more careful in his dress. He had metal buttons on his coat, wore better wigs, and at last bought a pair of silver buckles for his shoes, "at Wingman's, the well-known toy shop in St. James's Street, at the corner of St. James's Place." Boswell thinks the buckles were bought at Mrs. Thrale's suggestion. His walk was peculiar; he moved along with a rolling motion of the head and body, and sometimes indulged in strange gesticulations, but the description, given of these, was, probably, often exaggerated.

After his pension had given him the comforts afforded by a competent income, and constant visits to the Thrales had improved his health and spirits, many of his peculiarities had either disappeared, or were much diminished. But he could never get over his love of late hours, or, as Mrs. Piozzi put it, "his hatred of early ones." This kind and patient friend spoke from personal experience, as she had injured her own health by sitting up with him, when there was no one else to keep him company. "I lie down," said Johnson, "that my acquaintance may sleep, but I lie down to endure oppressive misery, and soon rise again to pass the night in anxiety and pain."

Another of Johnson's incurable weaknesses was an inordinate love of tea. In his review of Jonas Hanway's "Essay on Tea," he speaks of himself as "a hardened and shameless tea-drinker, who has for many years diluted his meals with only the infusion of this fascinating plant; whose kettle has scarcely time to cool; who with tea amuses the evening; with tea solaces the midnights, and with tea welcomes the morning." Cumberland records an occasion at his own house, when Sir Joshua ventured to remind Johnson that he had drunk eleven cups of tea. "Sir," replied he, "I did not count your glasses of wine, why should you number up my cups of tea? Sir, I should have released the lady from any further trouble if it had not been for your remark; but you have reminded me that I want one of the dozen, and I must request Mrs. Cumberland to round up my number."

It is unsafe to prophecy in literary matters, but there are many indications that Johnson's fame is destined to

last.   The extraordinary interest which he inspires is not
quite easy to account for, though it is, no doubt, a great
deal due to Boswell's delightful work, which is still widely
read, and, in some form or another, is constantly being
re-issued.   An excellent edition, prepared by the Rev.
Alexander Napier, was published in 1884, which contained all the information on the subject, which had come
to light since the days of Mr. Croker.   The " Reynolds
Edition," as it was called, appeared in 1885, edited by
Mr. Henry Morley, whose notes are of much greater value
than the engravings which illustrate the work.   At the
close of the last volume is a short essay, called " The Spirit
of Johnson," from the pen of the editor, which is one
of the best descriptions of his character that has ever
been written.   Another edition by Dr. George Birkbeck
Hill, an excellent Johnsonian scholar, is now passing
through the press.   But no reprint of Boswell can be of
any value that does not contain a large proportion of
Mr. Croker's notes.   It is impossible to exaggerate
the extent and value of the information collected by
that indefatigable editor, and a great many of his
anecdotes were obtained from sources now no longer
available.   Boswell's " Life " was fatal to the much less
amusing work by Sir John Hawkins, which had appeared
some years earlier.   This author was an extremely worthy
person, but dull and pompous, and his character can be
pretty well estimated from an epitaph by a contemporary
wit—

> " Here lies Sir John Hawkins
> In his shoes and stockings."

But he has received but scant justice, and his " Life of

Johnson " is spoken of with contempt by many who have never taken the trouble to do more than turn over its leaves. He was certainly, as Johnson said, an *unclubable* man, but the mere fact that he maintained the most intimate relations with Johnson for about thirty years, that Johnson, when dying, consulted him about testamentary arrangements, and appointed him an executor, shows that he must have had some sterling qualities. The members of the " Club " doubtless found him a bore, while he most likely had no very friendly feelings towards them, and it must have been a relief to all when he withdrew from that famous society. His knowledge of the obscure literary men of his day was very extensive, and his pages contain a great deal of interesting information about the Grub Street writers, with whom Johnson associated, when he first commenced his literary career. It is also valuable for the description of his early life in London ; and no one, who has not read it, can have a competent knowledge of the subject. Hawkins died before the publication of his rival's work, in which he was mentioned in no very flattering terms.

The first biography of Johnson is said to have appeared on the very day after his death. It was published by Kearsley without the author's name, as " The Life of Samuel Johnson, LL.D., with Occasional Remarks on his Writings. . . ." It is supposed to be written by a Mr. William Cooke, and contained much that was authentic. " The Memoirs of the Life and Writings of the Late Dr. Samuel Johnson " was published not long afterwards. It was also anonymous, but is attributed by Mr. Napier to a

Scotch clergyman, the Rev. William Shaw. The writer, whoever he may have been, must have had access to good sources of information, and the little volume is interesting. There are other biographies and essays, and some excellent magazine articles, of which a few derived a special value from their writers' personal knowledge of the subject. By far the best description of Johnson's death was given in a paper, contributed to *The European Magazine* of December, 1799, by Mr. Hoole, who was with him during his last illness.

Johnson, as just stated, owes a great deal to Boswell, but in any case his marked individuality, and even his eccentricities, made him a good subject for a biography. There is much that is attractive, and even picturesque, in his character. The strange contrast between his rugged, burly figure and the womanly tenderness of his heart, his manly self-respect, his haughty bearing in the presence of his superiors, his touching kindness and consideration to those who were the objects of his charity, and even his defects, such as his love of argument, his refusal to acknowledge defeat, his rudeness, sometimes expressed in quaint and unexpected turns of speech, all make up that striking and original figure which stands out in bold relief among his contemporaries.

In the present day Johnson derives a peculiar interest as a link between recent times and the early part of the eighteenth century. When quite a child, he was taken into the presence of Queen Anne, of whose personal appearance he had to the last a dim recollection, and, some seventy years later, he saw and conversed with the Prince of Wales, afterwards George IV., then a youth under the charge of Mrs. Percy. Johnson asked him what books he was reading, examined him in Scripture history, and was much pleased with the intelligence shown by the future king. Johnson had been brought into indirect communication with Pope and Swift. He must often have seen Walpole, Carteret, and Pulteney; and at the house of Henry Hervey, who married Catherine Aston, he might, perhaps, have met Pulteney's adversary in the famous duel, John Lord Hervey, the "Sporus" of Pope's "Satires," and the husband of Pope's friend, the beautiful Mary Lepel. And yet there are many still living, who have met those personally acquainted with Johnson. The present writer, in his schoolboy days, heard from an eye-witness a description of Johnson at a dinner party at the Thrales', and the narrator had a vivid recollection of his appearance and conversation. Martin Routh, the famous president of Magdalen College, Oxford, who survived till 1854, was probably the last person of note, who could speak of Johnson from personal recollection.

The centenary of Johnson's death occurred in December, 1884. There was no public, or formal, celebration of the event, but many of the newspapers and periodicals had articles alluding to the subject; and there was an interesting memorial service at St. Clement Danes, which Johnson, in his lifetime, was in the habit of attending. The empty pew in the gallery, where he used to sit, was draped in violet, and a cast of his bust, by Nollekens, was placed on the ledge in front. Those, who were present on the occasion, will not easily forget it, or the excellent practical address in which the rector, Dr. Lindsay, pointed out that the example of Johnson's career was not only intended for his contemporaries, but that those who came afterwards, and read the story of his life, might imitate his sturdy veracity, his uprightness, his consistency, and his blameless moral conduct.

THE END.

INDEX.

BIBLIOGRAPHY.

BY
JOHN P. ANDERSON
(British Museum).

I. WORKS.

The Works of Samuel Johnson, together with his life, and notes on his Lives of the Poets, by Sir J. Hawkins. 15 vols. London, 1787-9, 8vo.
   Originally published in 11 vols., the last 4 vols. being an addition.
——Another edition, with an Essay on his Life and Genius, by Arthur Murphy. 12 vols. London, 1792, 8vo.
——Another edition. 6 vols. Dublin, 1793, 8vo.
——Another edition, with an Essay on his life and genius, by Arthur Murphy. 12 vols. London, 1796, 8vo.
   Vol i. has a special title-page as follows: "An essay on the life and genius of S. J.," etc.
——Another edition. 12 vols. London, 1801, 8vo.
——Another edition. 12 vols. London, 1805, 8vo.

The Works of Samuel Johnson. Another edition. [Edited by A. Chalmers.] London, 1810, 8vo.
——Another edition. [Edited by A. Chalmers.] 12 vols. London, 1816, 12mo.
——Another edition. 11 vols. Oxford, 1825, 8vo.
   With half-titles, reading "Oxford English Classics," etc.
——Another edition. Edited by R. Lynam. 6 vols. London, 1825. 8vo.
——Another edition. 10 vols. London, 1818, 12mo.
——Another edition, in double columns. 2 vols. London, 1850, 8vo.

II. POETICAL WORKS.

The Poetical Works of S. J., now first collected, in one vol. London, 1785, 12mo.

The Poetical Works of S. J. Another edition. Dublin, 1785, 12mo.
——Another edition, enlarged. [Edited by G. Kearsley.] London, 1789, 8vo.
——Cooke's edition. London [1797 ?], 12mo.
The Poetical Works of S. J., to which is prefixed the life of the author. (*Anderson's Poets of Great Britain*, vol. xi.) Edinburgh, 1795, 8vo.
　The "Life" occupies pp. 779-836.
The Poetical Works of S. J., collated with the best editions: by Thomas Park. London, 1805, 16mo.
　In vol. 37 of "The Works of the British Poets," by Thomas Park. In vol. 6 of the Supplement some additional poems of S. J. are given.
The Poems of Dr. S. J., to which is prefixed a life of the author, by F. W. Blagdon. (*The Laurel.*) London, 1808, 24mo.
The Poems of S. J. (*Chalmers' Works of the English Poets*, vol. xvi) London, 1810, 8vo.
　With a Life of Johnson by Mr. Chalmers, pp. 549-570.
Select Poems of Dr. S. J., with a life of the author. ("The Works of the British Poets," edited by R. Walsh, vol. xxxi.) Philadelphia, 1822, 12mo.
The Poetical Works of Oliver Goldsmith, Tobias Smollett, Samuel Johnson, etc. Illustrated by John Gilbert. (*Routledge's British Poets.*) London, 1853, 8vo.
The Poetical Works of Johnson, Parnell, Gray and Smollett. With memoirs, critical dissertations, and explanatory notes, by the Rev. G. Gilfillan. Edinburgh, 1855, 8vo.

The Poetical Works of Johnson, etc. Another edition. The text edited by C. C. Clarke. London [1878], 8vo.
　Part of "Cassell's Library of British Poets."
The Poetical Works of Oliver Goldsmith, Tobias Smollett, S. J., etc. With biographical notices and notes. London [1881], 8vo.
London: a poem (by S. J.) in imitation of the third Satire of Juvenal. London, 1738, fol.
——Second edition. London, 1738, fol.
London: a poem. Fourth edition. London, 1739, fol.
The Vanity of Human Wishes. The tenth Satire of Juvenal, imitated by S. J. London, 1749, 4to.
Juvenal, translated by Charles Badham. With an appendix, containing imitations of the Third and Tenth Satires. By Dr. S. J. London, 1831, 16mo.
Dr. Johnson's Satires. London, and the Vanity of Human Wishes, with notes, historical and biographical, by I. P. Fleming. London, 1876, 16mo.
The Sixteenth Ode of the Third Book of Horace imitated [by S. J.]. London, 1777, 4to.

III. SELECTIONS.

The Beauties of Johnson. Consisting of maxims and observations, moral, critical, and miscellaneous, accurately extracted from the works of Dr. S. J., and arranged in alphabetical order. Enlarged. 2 vols. London, 1782, 12mo.
　Two other editions were published the same year.

The Beauties of Johuson. A new edition, being the seventh. The Beauties of S. J. To which are now added biographical anecdotes of the Doctor, etc. London, 1787, 12mo.

——The Beauties of S. J. To which are now added biographical anecdotes of the Doctor, selected from the works of Mrs. Piozzi, Mr. Boswell, and other testimonies; also the speech and sermon he wrote for Dr. Dodd. A new edition. London, 1828, 18mo.

——The Beauties of Johnson, consisting of selections from his works, by A. Howard. London [1834 ?], 12mo.

Deformities of Dr. S. J. Selected from his works. Edinburgh, 1782, 8vo.

——Second edition. London, 1782, 8vo.

The Life and Writings of S. J. [The life abridged from Gifford.] Selected and arranged by W. P. Page. 2 vols. New York, 1842-43, 12mo.

The Wisdom of the Rambler, Adventurer and Idler. By S. J. London, 1848, 16mo.

Wisdom and Genius of Dr. Samuel Johnson. Selected from his prose writings, by W. A. Clouston. (*Library of Thoughtful Books.*) London [1876], 8vo.

IV. SINGLE WORKS.

An Account of the Life of Mr. Richard Savage, etc. [By S. J.] London, 1744, 8vo.

——Second edition. London, 1748, 8vo.

The Life of Mr. R. Savage. The third edition, to which are added the Lives of Sir Francis Drake, and Admiral Blake, etc. [By S. J.] London, 1767, 8vo.

The Life of Mr. R. Savage. Fourth edition, etc. London, 1769, 8vo.

——Fourth edition. London, 1777, 12mo.

The Works of R. Savage, with an account of the life and writings of the author, by S. J. 2 vols. London, 1775, 8vo.

——Another edition. 2 vols. Dublin, 1777, 12mo.

An Account of the Life of S. J. from his birth to his eleventh year, written by himself; to which are added, original letters to Dr. S. J., by Miss H. Boothby; published from MSS. in the possession of R. Wright [the editor]. London, 1805, 8vo.

The celebrated Letter from S. J. to P. D. Stanhope, Earl of Chesterfield, now first published, with notes, by J. Boswell. London, 1790, 4to.

A Compleat Vindication of the Licensers of the Stage from the malicious and scandalous aspersions of Mr. Brooke. By an Impartial Hand [*i.e.*, S. J.] London, 1739, 4to.

A Conversation between His Most Sacred Majesty George III. and S. J. Illustrated with observations, by James Boswell. London, 1790, fol.

The Convict's Address, etc. [Written by Dr. J.] London, 1777], 8vo.

——Second edition. London, 1777, 8vo.

——Another edition. Salisbury, 1777, 12mo.

Thoughts in Prison, to which are added the Convict's Address, etc. Third edition. London, 1779, 12mo.

Debates in Parliament, by S. J. 2 vols. London, 1787, 8vo.

These two volumes are supplementary to all the collected editions of Johnson's works.

A Diary of a Journey into North Wales in 1774, edited, with illustrative notes [and an Itinerary of Wales,] by R. Duppa. (Appendix.) London, 1816, 8vo.

The Plan of a Dictionary of the English Language, addressed to the Right Hon. Philip Dormer, Earl of Chesterfield. London, 1747, 4to.

A Dictionary of the English Language, in which the words are deduced from their originals, and illustrated in their different significations by examples from the best writers. To which are prefixed a history of the language, and an English grammar. 2 vols. London, 1755, fol.

This is the original edition of Johnson's Dictionary, for which he received £1575 from the booksellers.

——Second edition. 2 vols. London, 1755, fol.

——Another edition. 2 vols. London, 1755, fol.

The copy in the British Museum Library formerly belonged to Edmund Burke.

——Another edition, abstracted from the folio edition, by the author. 2 vols. London, 1756, 8vo.

——Third edition. 2 vols. London, 1765, fol.

There is a copy of this edition in the British Museum Library with MS. additions and corrections in the autograph of Dr. J.

A Dictionary of the English Language. Fourth edition, revised by the author. 2 vols. London, 1773, fol.

——Fifth edition. 2 vols. London, 1773, 8vo.

——Fourth edition. 2 vols. Dublin, 1775, 4to.

One of the copies of this edition in the Library of the British Museum contains copious MS. notes and additions [by E. Malone].

——Sixth edition. 2 vols. London, 1778, 8vo.

——Sixth edition. 2 vols. London, 1785, 4to.

Among the numerous other editions are the following:—London, 1805, 8vo., with a Life of S. J. by J. Aikin; London, 1818, 4to, in 4 vols., with additions by H. J. Todd; London, 1855, 18mo, by P. A. Nuttall; London, 1866-70, 4to, in 2 vols., by R. G. Latham.

The False Alarm. [By S. J.] London, 1770, 8vo.

——Second edition. London, 1770, 8vo.

The Idler. [By S. J. and others.] 2 vols. London, 1761, 8vo.

Originally published in *The Universal Chronicle or Weekly Gazette.* No. i. appeared April 15, 1758; No. ciii. April 5, 1760.

——Another edition. 2 vols. London, 1795, 12mo.

——Another edition. (*Harrison's British Classicks*, vol. 8.) London, 1795, 8vo.

——Another edition. Cooke's edition, with engravings. London, 1799, 12mo.

——Another edition. London, 1807, 12mo.

——Another edition. (*British Classics*, vols. 23, 24.) 2 vols. London, 1810, 8vo.

——Another edition. (*The British Essayists*, by *A. Chalmers*, vol. 33.) London, 1817, 12mo.

The Idler. Another edition. (*The British Essayists*, by *A. Chalmers*, vol. 27.) London, 1823, 12mo.

——Another edition. (*The British Essayists*, by *James Ferguson*, vol. 19.) London, 1823, 12mo.

——Another edition. London, 1824, 12mo.

——Another edition. (*The British Essayists*, by *Lynam*, vol. 20.) London, 1827, 12mo.

——Another edition. (*The British Essayists*, by *A. Chalmers*, vol. 27.) Boston [U.S.], 1856, 8vo.

Irene; a tragedy [in five acts and in verse]. London, 1749, 8vo.

——Another edition. London, 1781, 8vo.

Irene; a tragedy [in five acts and in verse] as performed at the Theatre Royal, Drury Lane. (*Bell's British Theatre*, vol. 25.) London, 1796, 8vo.

Irene. (*Modern British Drama*, vol. 2.) London, 1811, 8vo.

A Journey to the Western Islands of Scotland. [By S. J.] London, 1775, 8vo.

——Another edition. Dublin, 1775, 8vo.

——Another edition. London, 1791, 8vo.

——Another edition. London, 1792, 12mo.

——Another edition. Edinburgh, 1798, 8vo.

——Another edition. Alnwick, 1800, 12mo.

——Another edition. Glasgow, 1811, 12mo.

——Another edition. London, 1816, 12mo.

——Another edition. Edinburgh, 1819, 12mo.

A Journey to the Western Islands of Scotland. Another edition, London, 1876, 8vo.

The Works of the English Poets. With prefaces, biographical and critical, by S. J. 68 vols. London, 1779-81, 8vo.

The Works of the Poets are in 56 vols., the Lives in 10, and the Index in 2, each series numbered separately.

——Another edition. 75 vols. London, 1790-80, 8vo.

The index in two vols. bearing date 1780, is part of, and adapted to, another edition.

——Prefaces, biographical and critical, to the Works of the English Poets. 10 vols. London, 1779-81, 12mo.

This, the first edition, forms under the title of prefaces a portion of the works of the English Poets in 68 vols. The first four vols. appeared in 1779. The greater number of the proof sheets, with S. J.'s MS. corrections, are in the South Kensington Museum.

The Works of the English Poets, with prefaces, biographical and critical, by Dr. S. J. 21 vols. London, 1810, 8vo.

The British Poets, including translations [and lives by S. Johnson, S. W. Singer, R. A. Davenport, and others]. 100 vols. Chiswick, 1822, 12mo.

The Lives of the most eminent English Poets, with critical observations on their works. 4 vols. London, 1781, 8vo.

——Another edition. 4 vols. London, 1783, 8vo.

There is an interleaved copy of this edition in the Library of the British Museum, with MS. Notes, by Sir Egerton Brydges, and another with some MS. Notes by the Rev Sir Herbert Croft, with two Autograph Letters to the same—viz., one by Dr. Johnson, and one by Mrs. Montagu.

The Lives of the most eminent English Poets. Another edition. 4 vols. London, 1790-91, 8vo.

——Another edition. 4 vols. London, 1793, 8vo.

——Another edition. 4 vols. Montrose, 1800. 12mo.

——Another edition. 3 vols. London, 1801, 8vo.

——Another edition. 7 vols. London, 1805-6, 16mo.

——Another edition. 3 vols. London, 1806, 8vo.

——Another Edition (*Encyclopædia of British Literature*, vol. 1). London, 1819. 8vo.

——Another edition. 2 vols. London, 1826, 12mo.

Part of a series entitled "Dove's English Classics." There is a second title-page, which is engraved.

——Another edition. London, 1840, 8vo.

——Another edition. Aberdeen, 1847, 12mo.

The copy in the Library of the British Museum contains copious MS. notes by J. D. Williams.

——Another edition, completed by W. Hazlitt. 4 vols. London, 1854, 8vo.

——Another edition, with notes corrective and explanatory, by P. Cunningham. 3 vols. London, 1854, 8vo.

——Another edition. (*Tauchnitz Edition*, vols. 418, 419.) Leipzig, 1858, 16mo.

——Another edition. 3 vols. Oxford [printed]. London, 1864-65, 18mo.

One of a series entitled "Oxford English Classics."

——Another edition. London, 1868, 8vo.

—— ——Johnson's Lives of the English Poets abridged, with notes and illustrations. To which is prefixed some account of Dr. Johnson. London, 1797. 12mo.

The Six Chief Lives from Johnson's "Lives of the Poets," with Macaulay's "Life of Johnson." Edited, with a preface, by M. Arnold. London, 1878, 8vo.

—— ——Another edition. London, 1886, 8vo.

—— ——The Life of I. Watts [extracted from Johnson's "Lives of the English Poets."] With notes, etc. London, 1785, 8vo.

—— ——The Lives of Dryden and Pope, with critical observations on their works. [Extracted from "The Lives of the English Poets."] Oxford, 1876, 12mo.

—— ——The Lives of Dryden, Pope, and Addison, etc. [Extracted from "The Lives of the English Poets."] Oxford, 1877, 12mo.

—— ——Poetical Works of John Dryden. [With Life by S. J.] 4 vols. London, 1811, 8vo.

The life comprises pp. i.-cxxiv., vol. i. The proof sheets b and f of J.'s Life of Dryden, with his MS. corrections, are in the Library of the British Museum.

—— ——Johnson. Select Works, edited, with introduction and notes, by Alfred Milnes. Lives of Dryden and Pope, and Rasselas. (*Clarendon Press Series*). Oxford, 1879, 8vo.

—— ——Johnson : Lives of Dryden and Pope. Edited, with introduction and notes, by Alfred Milnes. (*Clarendon Press Series.*) Oxford, 1885, 8vo.

—— ——Select British Poets; containing the entire works of Milton, Young, Thomson, etc. With lives (by S. Johnson) and portraits. 8 parts. London, 1810-08, 8vo.

Marmor Norfolciense; or, an essay on an ancient prophetical inscription, in monkish rhyme, lately discover'd near Lynn, in Norfolk. By Probus Britannicus [*i.e.*, Dr. S. Johnson]. London, 1739, 8vo.

——A new edition, with notes, and a Dedication to S. J., by Tribunus. Loudon, 1775, 8vo.

Memoirs of Charles Frederick, King of Prussia. (The first part written) by S. J., with notes and a continuation by Mr. Harrison. To which are added, translations of select poems written by the King of Prussia. London, 1786, 8vo.

Miscellaneous Observations on the Tragedy of Macbeth, with remarks on Sir T. H[anmer]'s edition of Shakespear. To which is affix'd Proposals for a new edition of Shakeshear [sic] with a specimen. [By S. J.] London, 1745, 12mo.

The Patriot. Addressed to the Electors of Great Britain. [By S. J.] London, 1774, 8vo.

——Third edition. London, 1775, 8vo.

Political Tracts [by S. J.] containing The False Alarm, Falkland's Islands, The Patriot, and Taxation no Tyranny. London, 1776, 8vo.

Prayers and Meditations composed by S. J. Published from his manuscripts by G. Strahan. London, 1785, 8vo.

——Second edition. London, 1785, 8vo.

——Another edition. London, 1806, 12mo.

——Another edition. London, 1813, 12mo.

Prayers and Meditations. Fifth edition. London, 1817, 8vo.

——Another edition. Glasgow, 1823, 12mo.

——Another edition. Glasgow, 1826, 12mo.

——Another edition. London, 1836, 24mo.

——Another edition; with a preface by W. Gresley. Lichfield, 1860, 8vo.

The Prince of Abissinia [*i.e.*, Rasselas]. A Tale, in two volumes. (First edition). London, 1759, 8vo.

This work has been translated into Bengalee, Dutch, French, German, Hungarian, Italian, Polish, Modern Greek, and Spanish.

——Second edition. 2 vols. London, 1759, 8vo.

——Another edition. 2 vols. Dublin, 1759, 8vo.

——Third edition. 2 vols. London, 1760, 12mo.

——Fifth edition. London, 1775, 12mo.

——Sixth edition. London, 1783, 12mo.

The History of Rasselas, Prince of Abissinia. A Tale. London, 1787, 8vo.

——Another edition. London, 1787, 12mo.

——Another edition. Edinburgh, 1789, 12mo.

——Ninth edition. London, 1793, 12mo.

——Another edition. London, 1794, 12mo.

——Another edition. 1795, 12mo.

——Another edition. [With illustrations.] London, 1801, 8vo.

——New mode of printing. Rasselas. Printed with patent types, in a manner never before attempted. Rusher's edition. Banbury, 1804, 8vo.

——Another edition. With engravings by A. Raimbach, from pictures by R. Smirke. London, 1805, 4to.
   This edition was republished in 1819.

——Rasselas, etc. (*Hunt's Classic Ta'es*, vol. 3.) London, 1806, 12mo.

——Another edition. London, 1807, 12mo.

——Another edition. Frederick-Town, 1810, 12mo.

Rasselas (*British Novelists*, vol. 26). London, 1810, 12mo.
   A notice on Johnson by Mrs. Barbauld, pp. i.-xiii. ; Rasselas, pp. 1-133.

——Another edition. London, 1812, 12mo.

——Another edition. Edinburgh, 1812, 12mo.

——Another edition. London, 1815, 24mo.

——Another edition. London, 1816, 12mo.

——Rasselas, a tale. Dinarbas : a tale : being a continuation of Rasselas [by E. C. Knight]. London, 1817, 12mo.

Rasselas [with a memoir of the author by Sir Walter Scott]. London, 1823, 8vo.
   Part of vol. v. of the " Novelists' Library."

——The History of Rasselas. By S. J. (*British Novelist*). London, 1823, 8vo.

——Another edition. London, 1835, 32mo.
   One of Tilt's *Miniature Classical Library.*

——Another edition. The Hague, 1838, 12mo.

——Another edition. Gouda, 1845, 8vo.

Rasselas. Rasselas and Select Poems. Edited by A. J. E., *i.e.*, A. J. Ellis. Phonetically Printed. [London] 1849, 16mo.

——Rasselas. (*Classic Tales*, etc.) London, 1852, 8vo.

——Another edition. London, 1855, 32mo.

——Another edition. London, 1858, 32mo.

——Another edition. London, 1860, 12mo.

——The Histori ov Raselas, etc. In the reportin stil ov Fonografi. London, 1867, 8vo.

Rasselas. (*Masterpieces of Fiction by Eminent Authors.*) London [1868], 8vo.

——Rasselas, etc. New York, 1869, 16mo.

——Another edition ; with an introduction, by the Rev. W. West. London, 1869, 16mo.

——Another edition. London, 1870, 32mo.

——Another edition. London [1879], 16mo.

——Another edition. London, 1880, 24mo.

——Classic Tales : comprising Johnson's Rasselas, etc. (*Bohn's Standard Library.*) London, 1882, 8vo.

——The Vicar of Wakefield, Rasselas, etc. With illustrations. London [1882], 8vo.

——The History of the Caliph Vathek, by William Beckford ; also Rasselas, Prince of Abyssinia, by S. J. London, 1883, 8vo.

——The History of Rasselas, etc. London, 1883, 18mo.

——Another edition. London [1883], 8vo.

——Another edition. London, 1884, 8vo.

Voltaire's Candide; or, the Optimist, and Rasselas, Prince of Abyssinia, by S. J. (*Morley's Universal Library.*) London, 1884, 8vo.

The Rambler. [By S. J.] 2 vols. London, 1750-52,·fol.

Commenced on Tuesday, March 20, 1749-50, and ended March 14, 1752. There are two copies in the Library of the British Museum; vols. i. and ii. of one copy are dated 1753, and vols. i. and ii. of the other, 1753, 1751 respectively.

——Another edition. 6 vols. London, 1752, 12mo.

——Another edition. 6 vols. Dublin, 1752, 12mo.

——Another edition. 4 vols. London, 1767, 12mo.

——Another edition. 4 vols. London, 1779, 12mo.

——Eleventh edition. 4 vols. London, 1789, 12mo.

——Another edition. (*Harrison's British Classicks*, vol. 1.) 4 vols. London, 1796, 8vo.

——Another edition. 4 vols. London, 1799-93, 12mo.

Vol. ii. is without a title-page; vols. iii. and iv. are dated 1793.

——Another edition. (*The British Classics*, vols. 15-18.) 4 vols. London, 1809, 8vo.

——Another edition. (*The British Essayists*, by *A. Chalmers*, vols. 19-22.) London, 1817, 12mo.

—— ——Vols. 16-18. London, 1823, 12mo.

—— ——Vols. 16-18. Boston [U. S.], 1856, 8vo.

—— ——Another edition. (*The British Essayists*, by *James Ferguson*, vols. 16-18.) London, 1823, 12mo.

——Another edition. (*The British Essayists*, by *Lynam*, vols. 12, 13.) London, 1827, 12mo.

The Rambler. Another edition. With a sketch of the author's life by Sir Walter Scott. 2 vols. London [1876], 8vo.

The Review of a Free Enquiry [by S. Jenyns] into the Nature and Origin of Evil [by S. Johnson.]. London, 1759, 8vo.

A Sermon [on John xi. 25, 26], written by the late S. J. for the funeral of his wife. Published by S. Hayes. London, 1788, 8vo.

Sermons on different subjects [attributed to S. Johnson], left for publication by John Taylor, LL.D. Published by S. Hayes. To which is added a sermon written by S. J. for the funeral of his wife. 2 vols. London, 1788-89, 8vo.

——Second edition. 2 vols. London, 1790-92, 8vo.

——Another edition. London, 1793, 8vo.

——Fourth edition. 2 vols. London, 1800, 8vo.

——Another edition. Walpole, N. H., 1806, 8vo.

——Fifth edition. London, 1812, 8vo.

Taxation no Tyranny; an Answer to the Resolutions and Address of the American Congress. [By S. J.] London, 1775, 8vo.

Thoughts on the late transactions respecting Falkland's Islands. [By S. J.]. London, 1771, 8vo.

A Voyage to Abyssinia, by Father Jerome Lobo. From the French [by S. J.]. London, 1735, 8vo.

This was the first prose work of Dr. Johnson. It was printed at Birmingham, and published anonymously.

A Voyage to Abyssinia, continued down to the beginning of the eighteenth century, with fifteen dissertations on various subjects. Translated from the French by S. J., etc. London, 1789, 8vo.

V. MISCELLANEOUS.

An account of an attempt to ascertain the longitude at sea, by an exact theory of the variation of the needle, etc. By Zachariah Williams. [Written by S. J.] London, 1755, 4to.

An account of the Life of John Philip Barretier, who was master of five languages at the age of nine years. [Written by S. J.] London, 1744, 8vo.
   Originally appeared in the *Gentleman's Magazine*, 1740-1742.

The Adventurer. [By Dr. John Hawkesworth, S. Johnson, and others.] 2 vols. London, 1753-54, fol.
   The first number of The Adventurer appeared on Nov. 7, 1752, and Johnson's first paper is dated March 3, 1753. It is stated that he contributed twenty-nine papers.

——Third edition. 4 vols. London, 1756, 12mo.

——Another edition. 2 vols. Dublin, 1760, 12mo.

——Fifth edition. London, 1766, 12mo.

——Another edition. 4 vols. London, 1770, 12mo.

——Another edition. 4 vols. London, 1778, 12mo.
   Numerous other Editions.

Catalogus Bibliothecæ Harleianæ. [By S. J., etc.] 5 vols. Londini, 1743-45, 8vo.

An account of the Harleian Library, pp. 1-8; Preface to the Catalogue, vol. iii., by S. J.

Christian Morals: by Sir Thomas Browne. With a Life of the Author, by S. J. Second edition. London, 1756, 12mo.

A Commentary, with Notes on the Four Evangelists and the Acts of the Apostles, etc, [With a Dedication to the King, and additions to the life by S. J.] By Zachary Pearce. 2 vols. London, 1777, 4to.

A complete system of Astronomical Chronology, unfolding the Scriptures. [With Dedication to the King, by S. J.] By John Kennedy. London, 1762, 4to.

A Dictionary of Ancient Geography, explaining the local appellations in Sacred, Grecian, and Roman History. [The Preface written by S. J.] By Alexander Macbean. London, 1773, 8vo.

A Dictionary of the English and Italian Languages, etc. [Dedication by S. J.] By Giuseppe Baretti. 2 vols. London, 1760, 4to.

Easy Phraseology, for the use of Young Ladies, etc. By Joseph Baretti. (Preface by S. J.) London, 1775, 8vo.

The English Works of Roger Ascham, etc., by James Bennet. [Life and Dedication by S. J.] London, 1761, 4to.

——Another edition. [With Life by S. J.] London, 1815, 8vo.

An Essay on Milton's use and imitation of the moderns, in his Paradise Lost. By William Lauder. [With a preface by S. J.] London, 1750, 8vo.

The Female Quixote; or, the Adventures of Arabella. [Dedication to the Earl of Middlesex by S. J.] By Charlotte Lennox. 2 vols. London, 1752, 12mo.

The Gentleman's Magazine for 1738. [Preface by S. J.] London, 1738, 8vo.

The Good Natur'd Man: A Comedy as performed at the Theatre Royal in Covent Garden. By Mr. Goldsmith. [Prologue written by S. J.] London, 1768, 8vo.

The Greek Theatre of Father Brumoy. Translated by Mrs. C. Lennox [assisted by Dr. S. J. etc.] 3 vols. London, 1759, 4to.

The Harleian Miscellany: a collection of scarce, curious, and entertaining pamphlets and tracts, etc. [Introduction written by S. J.] 8 vols. London, 1744-46, 4to.

An Introduction to the Game of Draughts. [The Dedication and Preface written by S. J.] By William Payne. London, 1756, 8vo.

Jerusalem Delivered, an heroic poem; translated from the Italian of Torquato Tasso, by John Hoole. [The Dedication to the Queen, written by S. J.] 2 vols. London, 1762, 8vo.

Letters to and from the late Samuel Johnson, etc. [Published by H. L. Piozzi]. 2 vols. London, 1788, 8vo.
There is a copy in the Library of the British Museum, with MS. Notes, by G. Baretti, and newspaper cuttings and engraved portraits of Johnson, Baretti, and Mr. Thrale inserted.

The Literary Magazine for 1756. [Preface by S. J.] London, 1756, 8vo.

London and Westminster improved, illustrated by plans, etc. [Dedication by S. J.] By John Gwynn. London, 1766, 4to.

A Medicinal Dictionary, including physic, surgery, anatomy, etc. [Dedication by S. J.] By Robert James. 3 vols. London, 1743-45, fol.

Miscellaneous and fugitive pieces [containing several acknowledged and anonymous writings of Dr. J.]. 3 vols. London, 1774, 8vo.

Miscellanies in prose and verse, by Anna Williams [including some pieces, with an advertisement, by Dr. J.]. London, 1766, 4to.

A Miscellany of Poems by several Hands. Published by J. Husbands, A.M., Fellow of Pembroke College, Oxon. Oxford, 1731, 8vo.
This work is rare, and is interesting, as it contains Dr. Johnson's first printed composition. Mr. Husbands, in his preface, says, "The translation of Mr. Pope's Messiah was delivered to his tutor as a college exercise by Mr. Johnson, a commoner of Pembroke College in Oxford, and 'tis hoped will be no discredit to the excellent original."

A New Dictionary of Trade and Commerce, compiled from the information of the most eminent merchants. [The Preface written by S. J.] By Mr. Rolt. London, 1756, fol.

A New Prologue, spoken by Mr. Garrick, April 5, 1750, at the representation of Comus, etc. [By S. J.] London, 1750, fol.

New Tables of Interest. [Preface by S. J.] By John Payne. London, 1758, obl. 16mo.

Original Letters from Richard Baxter, . . . Dr. S. Johnson,

etc. Edited by Rebecca Warner. Bath, 1817, 8vo.

Parliamentary Logick : by the Right Hon. W. G. Hamilton. With an appendix, containing considerations on the Corn Laws, by S. J. Never before printed. London, 1808, 8vo.

The Plays of William Shakespeare, with the corrections and illustrations of various Commentators. To which are added notes by [the editor] S. Johnson. 8 vols. London, 1765, 8vo.

Mr. Johnson's Preface to his edition of Shakespeare's Plays. London, 1765, 8vo.

The Preceptor, etc., by R. Dodsley. [With a Preface by Dr. J.] Vol. 1. London, 1748, 8vo. Numerous editions.

The Secretary, and complete letter writer; to which is added, An Essay on Letter Writing by Dr. S. J., and an Introduction to English Grammar. Birmingham, 1803, 12mo.

Shakespear illustrated; or the Novels and Histories on which the Plays of Shakespear are founded, etc. [With Dedication to John, Earl of Orrery, by S. J.] By the author of the Female Quixote [Charlotte Lennox]. 3 vols. London, 1753, 8vo.

Stenography; or Short-hand improved . . . By John Angel. [With Dedication by Dr. S. J.] London [1759 ?], 8vo.

Thoughts on the Coronation of his present Majesty King George the Third [with corrections and improvements by S. J.]. London, 1761, fol.

A Treatise describing and explaining the construction and use of new celestial and terrestrial globes, by George Adams. [With Dedication by S. J.] London, 1766, 8vo.

Westminster Abbey, with other occasional poems, and a free translation of the Œdipus Tyrannus [by T. Maurice; with a Preface by Dr. J.] London, 1813, 8vo.

A Word to the Wise, a Comedy, written by Hugh Kelly [with an address to the public by Dr. J.]. London, 1770, 8vo.

The World Displayed, or a curious collection of Voyages and Travels, selected from Writers of all Nations. [The Introduction written by S. J.] 20 vols. London, 1759, 12mo.

VI.—APPENDIX.

BIOGRAPHY AND CRITICISM.

Adelung, John C.—Three Philological Essays, chiefly translated from the German of J. C. A. by A. F. M. Willich. London, 1798, 8vo.
 The Third Essay "On the relative merits and demerits of Johnson's English Dictionary," pp. 169-186.

Agutter, Rev. William.—On the Difference between the deaths of the Righteous and the Wicked, illustrated in the instance of Dr. Samuel Johnson and David Hume. A Sermon, preached before the University of Oxford, at St. Mary's Church, July 23, 1786. London, 1800, 8vo.

Allibone, S. Austin.—A Critical Dictionary of English Literature, etc. 2 vols. Philadelphia, 1859, 8vo.
 Samuel Johnson, vol. I., pp. 971-982.

Anderson, Robert.—The Life of Samuel Johnson, with critical observations on his works. London, 1795, 8vo.
——Third edition. Edinburgh, 1815, 8vo.
Andrews, Samuel. — Our Great Writers; or, popular chapters on some leading authors. London, 1884, 8vo.
Samuel Johnson, pp. 188-206.
Bascom, John. — Philosophy of English Literature; a course of lectures delivered in the Lowell Institute. New York, 1874, 8vo.
Johnson, pp. 199-203.
Blackburne, F. — Remarks on Johnson's Life of Milton [by F. Blackburne], etc. London, 1780, 16mo.
Biographical Magazine.—Lives of the Illustrious. (*The Biographical Magazine.*) Vol. 4. London, 1853, 8vo.
Samuel Johnson, pp. 1-12.
Bolton, Sarah K.—Lives of Poor Boys who became famous. New York [1886], 8vo.
Dr. Samuel Johnson, with portrait, pp. 83-89.
Boswell, James.—The Journal of a Tour to the Hebrides with Samuel Johnson, LL.D., containing some poetical pieces relative to the Tour, a Series of his Conversation, etc. London, 1785, 8vo.
——Second edition, revised, etc. London, 1785, 8vo.
——Third edition, revised, etc, London, 1786, 8vo.
——Fifth edition. London, 1812, 12mo.
——Sixth edition. London, 1813, 8vo.
For other editions of the Journal of a Tour to the Hebrides, see "The Life of S. Johnson," by Boswell.

Boswell, James.—Pindar, Peter, *pseud.* [*i.e.,* J. Wolcot]. A Poetical and Congratulatory Epistle to J. B., on his Journal of a Tour to the Hebrides, etc. 1876. 4to.
Several Editions.
—— ——Verax. Remarks on the Journal of a Tour to the Hebrides, in a letter to J. B., Esq. [Signed Verax]. [1785] 8vo.
—— ——A Defence of Mr. Boswell's Journal, in a Letter to the Author of the Remarks, etc. London, 1786, 8vo.
—— ——The Remarker remarked, or a Parody on the Letter to Mr. Boswell, on his Tour, etc. London, 1786, 8vo.
—— ——[Twenty Caricatures by T. Rowlandson, in illustration of Boswell's Journal of a Tour to the Hebrides.] [London], 1786, fol.
Originally published in paper wrappers (now very rare) with the title "Picturesque Beauties of Boswell."
——The Life of Samuel Johnson, LL.D., comprehending an account of his studies and numerous works in chronological order; a series of his Epistolary Correspondence and Conversations, and various original pieces of his composition never before published, etc. 2 vols. London, 1791, 4to.
—— ——The principal Corrections and Additions to the first edition of Mr. Boswell's Life of Dr. Johnson. London, 1793, 4to.
——Second edition, revised and augmented. 3 vols. London, 1793, 8vo.
——Third edition, augmented. 4 vols. London, 1799, 8vo.

Boswell, James.—Fourth edition, augmented. 4 vols. London, 1804, 8vo.

——Fifth edition, augmented. 4 vols. London, 1807, 8vo.
The copy in the Library of the British Museum contains a few MS. Notes by Malone and Haslewood.

——Sixth edition, augmented. 4 vols. London, 1811, 8vo.

——Seventh edition, augmented. 5 vols. London, 1811, 12mo.

——Eighth edition, augmented. 4 vols. London, 1816, 8vo.

——Another edition. 4 vols. London, 1819, 12mo.

——Another edition. 4 vols. London, 1822, 8vo.

——Another edition. 4 vols. Oxford, 1826, 8vo.
Forms part of the "Oxford English Classics."

——Another edition. With copious notes and biographical illustrations by E. Malone. London, 1830, 8vo.

——The Life of S. J., including a Journal of a Tour to the Hebrides by J. B. A new edition, with numerous additions and notes by J. Wilson Croker. 5 vols. London, 1831, 8vo.
Mr. Croker has reprinted Malone's Notes to his edition of the Life, and has incorporated with the present work Mrs. Piozzi's Anecdotes of Dr. Johnson, Dr. Johnson's Tour in Wales, edited with notes by R. Duppa, and Courtenay's poetical Review of the character of Dr. Johnson.

——Another edition. To which are added Anecdotes by Hawkins, Piozzi, Murphy, Tyers, Reynolds, Steevens, etc., and notes by various hands (E. Malone, A. Chalmers, J. Wilson Croker, etc.). 10 vols. London, 1835, 8vo.

Boswell, James.—Another edition, revised, with much additional matter. By J. Wilson Croker. London, 1848, 8vo.

——The Life of S. J. (The Journal of a Tour to the Hebrides, with introduction and notes by R. Carruthers. A new edition, illustrated, etc. (*National Illustrated Library.*) 5 vols. London [1851-2], 8vo.

——Another edition. By J. Wilson Croker, revised and enlarged by J. Wright. Illustrated with engravings, etc. (Johnsoniana: a collection of miscellaneous anecdotes and sayings of Dr. S. J., etc.) (*Bohn's Shilling Series.*) 10 vols. London, 1859, 8vo.

——Another edition. By J. Wilson Croker. With portraits. 10 pts. London, 1860, 8vo.

——The Life of S. J. Edited, with copious notes, by E. Malone. Unabridged edition. London [1865], 8vo.

——A new edition, elucidated by copious notes. With illustrations by J. Portch. London, 1867, 8vo.

——Another edition. Edited by E. Malone. Unabridged edition. London [1868], 8vo.

——Another edition. (*Blackwood's Universal Library of Standard Authors.*) London [1872], 8vo.

——New edition, revised. Edited, with notes, by W. Wallace. Edinburgh, 1873, 8vo.

——The Life of S. J. Together with a Journal of a Tour to the Hebrides. A reprint of the first edition. To which are added Mr. Boswell's corrections and additions, issued in 1792; the variations of the second edition, with some of the author's notes prepared for the third : the whole edited, with new notes, by Percy Fitzgerald, etc. 3 vols. London, 1874, 8vo.

——New edition. By J. Wilson Croker. With portraits. London, 1876, 8vo.

——The Life of S. J., including a Journal of a Tour to the Hebrides. 3 vols. London [1883], 8vo.

——The Life of Samuel Johnson, LL.D. Together with the Journal of a Tour to the Hebrides. New editions, with notes and appendices by A. Napier. (Johnsoniana : Anecdotes of Samuel Johnson by Mrs. Piozzi and others; together with the diary of Dr. Campbell and extracts from that of Madame D'Arblay. Newly collected and edited by A. Napier.) 5 vols. London, 1884, 8vo.
Vol. 5 is not numbered, but issued as an appendix to vols. i.-iv.

——Another edition. 6 vols. London, 1884, 8vo.

——Centenary edition. London [1884], 8vo.

——The Life of Dr. Samuel Johnson, carefully abridged from Mr. Boswell's large work. By F. Thomas, Esq. London, 1792, 12mo.

——The Life of S. J., chiefly compiled from "Boswell's Johnson." By M. A. Donne. Published under the direction of the Society for Promoting Christian Knowledge. London [1863], 16mo.

——Life and Conversation of Dr. S. J. (founded chiefly upon Boswell). By A. Main. With a preface by G. H. Lewes. London, 1874, 8vo.

The Life of S. J., comprising an account of his studies and numerous works, etc. [Abridged from Boswell's "Life of S. J.," etc.] Otley [1877], 16mo.

—— ——"Extracts from the Monthly Review" of London, accompanied by Boswell's Life of Dr. Johnson. [Proposals, by Messrs. Andrews and Blake, for publishing a new edition of the Life, criticising the work.] [Charlestown, Mass., 1807], 8vo.

—— ——Answers to Mr. Macaulay's Criticism in the Edinburgh Review on Mr. Croker's edition of Boswell's Life of Johnson. Selected from Blackwood's Magazine. London, 1856, 8vo.

—— ——Boswell again, etc. [A defence of J. B. against Macaulay's attack in his review of the Life of Johnson.] By Philalethes. London, 1878, 8vo.

——A Letter to James Boswell, Esq., with some Remarks on Johnson's Dictionary and on Language, etc. London, 1792, 8vo.

——Epistle to James Boswell, Esq. ; occasioned by his long expected and now speedily to be published Life of Dr. Johnson. London, 1790, 4to.

——Johnsoniana; or, Supplement to Boswell; being Anecdotes and Sayings of Dr. Johnson, etc. London, 1836, 8vo.

——Another edition. 2 vols. London, 1848, 12mo.

——Another edition. 2 vols. London, 1859, 12mo.

——Boswelliana. The Commonplace Book of J. Boswell. With a Memoir and Annotations by

the Rev. Charles Rogers, etc. London, 1874, 8vo.
Printed for the Grampian Club.

British Poets. Biographical Sketches of Eminent British Poets, etc. Dublin, 1851, 8vo.
Samuel Johnson, pp. 326-349.

Brough, William. — Rasselas, Prince of Abyssinia; or, the Happy Valley. An Extravaganza founded on Dr. Johnson's well-known tale, etc. London [1863], 12mo.
In vol. 57 of "Lacy's Acting Edition of Plays."

Brougham, *Lord.*—Lives of Men of Letters and Science, who flourished in the time of George III. 2 vols. London, 1846, 8vo.
Johnson, with portrait, vol. ii., pp. 1-85.

——Works of Henry, Lord Brougham. Edinburgh, 1872, 8vo.
Johnson, vol. ii., pp. 304-377.

Buckland, Anna.—The Story of English Literature. London, 1882, 8vo.
Samuel Johnson and his friends, pp. 442-457.

Burney, afterwards D'Arblay, Frances. — Diary and Letters. 7 vols. London, 1832-46, 8vo.
Contains numerous anecdotes of, and references to Dr. Johnson.

Campbell, Archibald. — Lexiphanes, a dialogue imitated from Lucian. Being an attempt to expose the hard words of our English Lexiphanes, the Rambler [S. J.]. By A. Campbell. London, 1767, 12mo.

Carlyle, Thomas. — Biographical Essays. by T. C. No. 1, Samuel Johnson. London, 1853, 8vo.

——Critical and Miscellaneous Essays, etc. 6 vols. London [1885], 8vo.
Boswell's Life of Johnson, vol. iv., pp. 25-106. Reprinted from *Fraser's Magazine*, vol. v.

Cary, Henry Francis. Lives of English Poets, from Johnson to Kirke White, designed as a continuation of Johnson's Lives. London, 1846, 8vo.
Samuel Johnson, pp. 1-93.

Clark, F. L.—Golden Friendships, etc. London, 1884, 8vo,
Dr. Johnson and Goldsmith, pp. 74-91.

Courtenay, John. — A Poetical Review of the Literary and Moral Character of the late S. J. With Notes. London, 1786, 4to.

Craik, George L.—A Compendious History of English Literature, etc. 2 vols. London, 1861, 8vo.
Johnson, vol. ii., pp. 306-310.

——A Manual of English Literature, etc. Ninth edition. London [1883], 8vo.
Johnson, pp. 404-408.

Cunningham, George Godfrey.— The English Nation; a History of England, with Lives of Englishmen. 5 vols. Edinburgh [1863-68], 4to.
Samuel Johnson, vol. iv., pp. 208-220, with portrait.

Dawson, George. — Biographical Lectures, by George Dawson, M.A. London, 1886, 8vo.
Dr. Samuel Johnson, pp. 159-171.

Drake, Nathan. — Essays, biographical, critical, and historical, illustrative of the Rambler, Adventurer, and Idler, etc. 2 vols. Buckingham, *printed.* London, 1809-10, 16mo.
The Literary Life of Dr. J., vol. i., pp. 111-499.

Drake, Samuel Adams.—Our Great

Benefactors ; short biographies, etc. Boston [U.S.], 1884, 4to.
Samuel Johnson, illustrated, pp. 43-46.

Dulcken, H. W.—Worthies of the World, a series of historical and critical sketches, etc. London [1881], 8vo.
Dr. Samuel Johnson, with portrait, pp. 97-112.

Dumont (de Monteux).—Lettre à Mons. A Latour sur l'état pathologique de Samuel Johnson. (*L'Union Medicale*, tom. xi., 1857, pp. 297-298, and 321-323.)

Duyckinck, Evert A. — Portrait Gallery of Eminent Men and Women, etc. New York [1875], 4to.
Samuel Johnson, with portrait, vol. i., pp. 5-27.

Encyclopædia Britannica.—Encyclopædia Britannica. Eighth edition. Edinburgh, 1853-60, 4to.
Article Johnson, by Lord Macaulay, vol. xii., pp. 793-804; reprinted in the 9th edition.

Essay.—An Essay upon the King's Friends, with an account of some discoveries made in Italy, and found in a Virgil, concerning the Tories. To Dr. S——l J——n. London. 1776, 8vo.

Essays. — Critical and Miscellaneous Essays. By an Octogenarian. 2 vols. Cork, 1851, 8vo.
Johnson, his contemporaries and biographers, pp. 312-348.

Fitzgerald, Percy. — Croker's Boswell and Boswell. Studies in the Life of Johnson. London, 1880, 8vo.

Fordyce, James.—Addresses to the Deity. London, 1785, 8vo.
Address VI., On the Death of Dr. Samuel Johnson, pp. 209-232.

Francis, *Barber.*—More last words of Dr. J., consisting of important and valuable anecdotes, etc. London, 1787, 8vo.

Frost, John.—Lives of Eminent Christians. Philadelphia, 1852. 8vo.
S. Johnson, pp. 323-331.

Gilfillan, George. — Galleries of Literary Portraits. 2 vols. Edinburgh, 1857, 8vo.
Dr. Johnson, vol. ii. pp. 217-226.

Gisborne, Thomas. — Reflections on recent occurrences at Lichfield ; including an illustration of the opinions of S. J. on Slavery, etc. London, 1826, 8vo.

Hacho, *King.*—The fatal effects of Luxury and Indolence, exemplified in the History of Hacho, King of Lapland. A tale of Dr. S. Johnson's versified. Chesterfield, 1778, 4to.

Hawkins, Sir John.—The Life of Samuel Johnson, by Sir John Hawkins. London, 1787, 8vo.
——Second edition corrected. London, 1787, 8vo.
——Another edition. Dublin, 1787, 8vo.

Hawthorne, Nathaniel. — Tales, Sketches, and other papers, by N. Hawthorne. Boston [U.S.], 1883, 8vo.
Samuel Johnson, pp. 166-176.

Hazlitt, William. — Johnson's Lives of the British Poets, completed by W. H. 4 vols. London, 1854, 8vo.
Samuel Johnson, illustrated, pp. 70-93.

Hazlitt, W. Carew.—Offspring of Thought in Solitude. Modern Essays. London, 1884, 8vo.
Essay on Dr. Johnson, pp. 47-56.

Henderson, Andrew.—A Letter to Dr. Samuel Johnson, on his Journey to the Western Isles, etc London [1775], 8vo.

Henderson, Andrew.—A Second Letter to Dr. S. J., in which his wicked and opprobrious invectives [in his "Journey to the Hebrides"] are shewn, etc. London [1775], 8vo.

Hewlett, J. T.—Dr. Johnson : his religious life and his death. By the author of "Dr. Hookwell," etc. London, 1850, 12mo.

Hill, George Birkbeck. — Dr. Johnson, his friends and his critics. London, 1878, 8vo.

Hobhouse, Thomas.—Elegy to the Memory of Doctor Samuel Johnson. London, 1785, 4to.

Howe, J., Lord Chedworth.— Notes upon some of the obscure passages in Shakespeare's plays; with remarks upon the explanations and amendments of the commentators in the editions of 1785, 1790, 1793 [Dr. Johnson, G. Steevens, etc.]. London, 1805, 8vo.

Hutton, Laurence. — Literary Landmarks of London. London [1885], 8vo.
   Samuel Johnson, pp. 155-171.

Ivimey, Joseph.—John Milton, his life and times ; with an appendix containing animadversions upon Dr. J.'s Life of Milton, etc. London, 1833, 8vo.

Johnson, Samuel.—A letter to S. J. [in reply to "The False Alarm"]. [London] 1770, 8vo.

——The Constitution defended, and Pensioner exposed ; in remarks on the "False Alarm." [A pamphlet by Dr. J.] London, 1770, 8vo.

——History and Defence of Magna Charta. London, 1772, 8vo.
   This work was not written by Samuel Johnson, although his name appears on the title-page.

Johnson, Samuel.—Magna Charta, with its history and defence. With the Bill of Rights, Scots' Claim of Rights, Habeas Corpus Act, and an introductory discourse, with an essay on Parliaments. Edinburgh, 1794, 12mo.

——The Pamphlet, entitled "Taxation no Tyranny" [by S. J.], candidly considered, and its arguments and pernicious doctrines exposed and refuted. London [1775,] 8vo.

——Tyranny Unmasked ; an answer to a late pamphlet, entitled Taxation no Tyranny [by S. J.]. London, 1775, 8vo.

——An Answer to a Pamphlet, entitled Taxation no Tyranny, addressed to the Author [S. J.]. London, 1775, 8vo.

——Taxation, Tyranny. Addressed to S. Johnson, LL.D. London, 1775, 8vo.

——Remarks on the Patriot. [A pamphlet by S. J.] Including some hints respecting the Americans ; with an address to the Electors of Great Britain. London, 1775, 8vo.

——Remarks on a Voyage to the Hebrides, in a Letter to S. J. London, 1775, 8vo.

——Johnsoniana ; or, a Collection of Bon Mots by Dr. Johnson and others. Together with the choice sentences of Publius Syrus. Now first translated into English. London, 1776, 12mo.

——A Cursory Examination of Dr. Johnson's Strictures on the Lyric performances of Gray. London, 1781, 8vo.

——Remarks on Dr. Johnson's Life, and critical observations

on the works of Mr. Gray. London, 1782, 8vo.

——Observations on Dr. Johnson's life of Hammond. London; 1782, 4to.

——Remarks on Dr. Johnson's Lives of the most eminent Poets. By a Yorkshire Freeholder. London, 1782, 4to.

——A Criticism on the Elegy written in a Country Churchyard. Being a continuation of Dr. J.'s Criticism on the Poems of Gray. London, 1783, 8vo. Attributed to Mr. Young, Professor of Greek, Glasgow.

——Second edition. Edinburgh, 1810, 8vo.

Ode by Dr. S. Johnson to Mrs. Thrale upon their supposed approaching nuptials. [A satire.] London, 1784, 4to.

——A Dialogue between Dr. Johnson and Dr. Goldsmith, in the shades, relative to the former's Strictures on the English Poets, particularly Pope, Milton, and Gray. London, 1785, 4to.

——Johnson's Laurel; or, Contest of the Poets; a poem. London, 1785, 4to.

——Memoirs of the Life and Writings of S. J., containing original letters and anecdotes both of his literary and social connections. London, 1785, 8vo.

——The Life of S. J., with occasional Remarks on his Writings, an authentic copy of his Will, and a Catalogue of his Works; to which are added some papers written by Dr. J. in behalf of a late unfortunate character [Dr. Dodd] never before published. London, 1785, 8vo.

——An Ode on the much-lamented Death of Dr. Samuel Johnson. Written the 18th of December 1784. London, 1785, 4to.

——Verses on the Death of Dr. Samuel Johnson. London, 1785, 4to.

——A poetical epistle from the ghost of Dr. Johnson to his four friends : The Rev. Mr. Strahan, J. Boswell, Esq., Mrs. Piozzi, J. Courtenay, Esq., M.P., from the original copy in the possession of the editor. With notes, critical, biographical, historical, and explanatory. London, 1786, 4to.

——A Monody on the much-lamented Death of Samuel Johnson, LL.D. By the author of the Field Negroe, etc. London, 1786, 4to.

——Anecdotes of the Learned Pig, with notes, critical and explanatory ; and illustrations, from Bozzy, Piozzi, etc. London, 1786, 4to.

A Critical Review of the Works of S. J., containing a particular vindication of several eminent characters. London, 1783, 8vo.

——Another edition. London, 1787, 8vo.

——Letter to Dr. Johnson on the subject of a Future State, by — Taylor. — 1787.

——The Art of Criticism ; as exemplified in Dr. Johnson's Lives of the most eminent English Poets. London, 1789, 8vo.

Reflections on the last scene of the late Dr. Johnson's Life ; as exhibited by his biographer,

13

Sir John Hawkins; also
Thoughts on the Millennium.
London, 1791, 8vo.
——The Witticisms, Anecdotes,
Jests, and Sayings of Dr. S.
Johnson, collected from Boswell
and other gentlemen. And a
full account of Dr. J.'s con-
versation with the King [George
III.]. To which is added a
number of jests, by J. Merry.
London, 1791, 8vo.
   With an engraving by R. Cruik-
shanks, father of George Cruik-
shank, entitled "Mrs. Thrale's
Breakfast Table." The copy in the
Library of the British Museum has
an additional plate by J. Roberts,
with the title, "Dr. Johnson's En-
tertainment at a Highland Change,"
and also some newspaper cuttings.
——Second edition, improved.
London, 1793, 8vo.
——Third edition, etc. London,
1797, 8vo.
——The Character of Dr. J.
With illustrations from Mrs.
Piozzi, Sir John Hawkins, and
Mr. Boswell. London, 1792,
8vo.
——Dr. Johnson's Table Talk,
containing Aphorisms, Anec-
dotes, etc., selected from Bos-
well's Life of Johnson. London,
1798, 8vo.
——Another edition. London,
1825, 12mo.
——The Table Talk of S. J.
Edinburgh [1868], 16mo.
——A Dialogue between Dr. J.
and Mrs. Knowles. [On the
Christianity of the Society of
Friends.] London, 1799, 8vo.
   Appeared originally in the Gentle-
man's Magazine, June 1791.
——A Critical Inquiry into the
Moral Writings of Dr. Samuel
Johnson; to which is added a
Dialogue in the Shades between

Johnson and Boswell. London,
1802, 8vo.
——Two New Dialogues of the
Dead, the first between Handel
and Braham, the second between
Johnson and Boswell. London,
1804, 8vo.
——The Life of Dr. Johnson.
(*Select Biography*, vol. 6).
London, 1821, 12mo.
——Graphic Illustrations of the
life and times of Samuel
Johnson. London, 1837, 4to.
——Dr. Johnson on his Death-
bed. [A religious tract.] Bir-
mingham [1855 ?], s.sh. 8vo.
Kenrick, William.—An Epistle to
James Boswell, Esq., occasioned
by his having transmitted the
moral writings of Dr. S. J. to
Pascal Paoli, General of the
Corsicans, etc. By W. K. [*i.e.*,
William Kenrick]. London,
1768, 8vo.
——A Review of Dr. Johnson's
new edition of Shakespeare; in
which the ignorance, or inatten-
tion of that editor is exposed,
etc. London, 1765, 8vo.
Knox, John.—Extracts from the
publications of Mr. Knox, Dr.
Anderson, Mr. Pennant, and Dr.
Johnson, relative to the Northern
and North-Western Coasts of
Great Britain. London, 1787,
8vo.
Lady.—A Journey to the High-
lands of Scotland; with occasional remarks on Dr. Johnson's
Tour, by a Lady. London
[1776 ?], 8vo.
Macaulay, T. B.—Biographies by
Lord Macaulay, contributed to
the Encyclopædia Britannica,
etc. Edinburgh, 1860, 8vo.
Samuel Johnson, pp. 77-135.

Macaulay, T. B., The Works of T. B. M. 8 vols. London, 1866, 8vo.

Samuel Johnson [An Essay on Croker's edition of Boswell's Life of Johnson], vol. v., pp. 498-538; Life of Samuel Johnson, vol. vii., pp. 324-356. Originally appeared in the Edinburgh Review, 1857, and in the Encyclopædia Britannica, 1856, respectively.

McNicol, Donald—Remarks on Dr. Samuel Johnson's Journey to the Hebrides, etc. London, 1779, 8vo.

Mason, E. T.—Samuel Johnson, his words and his ways, etc. Edited by E. T. M. New York, 1879, 8vo.

Mason, George.—A Supplement to Johnson's English Dictionary; of which the palpable errors are attempted to be rectified, and its material omissions supplied. By George Mason. London, 1801, 4to.

——A Review of the Proposals of the Albion Fire Insurance; also a narrative of gross misbehaviour towards the public in the British Critic, on the subject of the appendix to the supplement to J.'s Dictionary. London, 1806, 8vo.

Maxwell, Robert.—A Letter from a Friend in England to Mr. Maxwell, with a character of Mr. Johnson's English Dictionary lately published, etc. Dublin, 1755, 4to.

Mézières, L.—Histoire Critique de la Littérature Anglaise, etc. Seconde édition. 3 tom. Paris, 1841, 8vo.

Johnson, tom. ii., pp. 28-131.

Milnes, Richard Monckton, *Lord Houghton.*—Boswelliana. London, 1855-6, 8vo.

No. 15, vol. ii. of the "Miscellanies of the Philobiblon Society."

Minto, William. — A Manual of English Prose Literature, etc. Edinburgh, 1872, 8vo.

Samuel Johnson, pp. 474-492.

——Another edition. London, 1881, 8vo.

Samuel Johnson, pp. 409-424.

Mitford, Mary Russell. — Recollections of a literary life; or, books, places, and people. 3 vols. London, 1852, 8vo.

Samuel Johnson, pp. 200-225.

Montagu, Basil.—Enquiries respecting the Insolvent Debtors' Bill, with the opinions of Dr. Paley, Mr. Burke, and Dr. Johnson, upon Imprisonment for Debt. By Basil Montagu. (The Pamphleteer, vol. 5., 1815, pp. 513-542).

——Enquiries respecting the Insolvent Debtors' Bill, with the opinions of Dr. Paley, Mr. Burke, and Dr. Johnson, upon Imprisonment for Debt. Second edition. London, 1816, 8vo.

Mudford, William.—A Critical Examination of the Writings of Richard Cumberland, Esq., with an occasional inquiry into the age in which he lived, etc. 2 vols. London, 1812, 8vo.

References to S. Johnson in vol. i.

Murphy, Arthur.—An Essay on the Life and Genius of S. Johnson. London, 1792, 8vo.

——Another edition. London, 1793, 8vo.

Nicoll, Henry J.—Landmarks of English Literature. London, 1883, 8vo.

Samuel Johnson, pp. 235-249.

Notes and Queries. General Index to Notes and Queries. Five series. London, 1856-1880, 4to.

Numerous references to S. J.

Olla Podrida. The Olla Podrida, a periodical work, etc. London, 1788, 8vo.
An Essay on Johnson, by Dr. Horne, Bishop of Norwich, No. 13, pp. 132-141.

Parley, Peter, *i.e.,* Samuel Griswold Goodrich.—Famous Men of Modern Times, etc. (*Parley's Cabinet Library,* vol. i.) Philadelphia, 1846, 8vo.
Samuel Johnson, pp. 207-227.

Penny, Anne. — Anningait and Ajutt; a Greenland Tale. Inscribed to Mr. Samuel Johnson. Taken from the 10th volume of his Ramblers, versified by a Lady [*i.e.,* Anne Penny]. London, 1861, 4to.

People. — Famous People and Famous Places. London [1883], 8vo.
Dr. Johnson and Mrs. Thrale, pp. 43-59.

People's Art Union.—The People's Art Union. The Historic Gallery of Portraits and Paintings, etc. London [1871]. 8vo.
Dr. Johnson, vol. iii., pp. 178-188.

Perry, Thomas Sergeant.—English Literature in the Eighteenth Century. New York, 1883, 8vo.
Johnson, pp. 403-415.

Phillips, Maude G.—A Popular Manual of English Literature, etc. 2 vols. New York, 1885, 8vo.
Characteristics of the Johnsonian Age, vol. ii., pp. 3-84, with portrait of Dr. Johnson.

Pindar, Peter *i.e.,* John Wolcot.— Bozzy and Piozzi; or, the British biographers; a town eclogue. By Peter Pindar. London, 1786, 4to.
Numerous editions.

Poole, John.—Hamlet Travestie, in three acts, with [burlesque] annotations by Dr. Johnson and Geo. Steevens, Esq., etc. London [1853], 12mo.
In Vol. x. of Lacy's "Acting Edition of Plays"

Potter, R.—An Inquiry into some passages in Dr. Johnson's Lives of the Poets: particularly his observations on Lyric poetry, and the Odes of Gray. London, 1783, 4to.

R. R.—A defence of Mr. Kenrick's Review of Dr. Johnson's Shakespeare; containing a number of curious and ludicrous anecdotes of literary biography. By a Friend. London, 1766, 8vo.

Regulus, *pseud.*—A defence of the resolutions and address of the American Congress in reply to Taxation no Tyranny [a pamphlet by S. J.]. London [1775], 8vo.

Reynald, H.—Samuel Johnson. Étude sur sa vie et sur ses principaux ouvrages, par H. R. Paris, 1856, 8vo.

Reynolds, Sir Joshua.—Johnson and Garrick. [Not published.] Jeu d'esprit written to illustrate a remark "That Dr. Johnson considered Garrick as his property, and would never suffer anyone to praise or abuse him but himself." London, 1816, 8vo.
The British Museum possesses the copy presented to Mrs. Siddons by the Marchioness of Thomond.

Richardson, Charles. — Illustrations of English Philology; consisting of a Critical Examination of Dr. Johnson's Dictionary, etc. London, 1815, 4to.
——Another edition. London, 18 26, 4to.

Ross, George. — Studies : biographical and literary. London, [1867], 8vo.
  Dr. Johnson, pp. 63-118.

Russell, J. F.—The Life of Dr. Samuel Johnson. London, 1847, 8vo.

Servois, Jean Pierre.—Notice sur la vie et les ouvrages du Docteur S. Johnson. Cambrai, 1823, 8vo.

Seymour, E. H.—Remarks, critical, conjectural, and explanatory, upon the plays of Shakespeare ; resulting from a collation of the early copies, with that of Johnson and Steevens, etc. 2 vols. London, 1805, 8vo.

Simeon, Sir John.—Miscellanies of the Philobiblon Society. London, 1860-1, 8vo.
  Vol. vi. contains "Original Letters of Dr. Johnson," communicated by Sir John Simeon.

Simpson, Joseph.—The Patriot, a tragedy from a manuscript of the late Dr. S. Johnson [or rather Joseph Simpson], corrected by himself. London, 1785, 8vo.

Squibb, George James.—Last illness and post-mortem examination of Samuel Johnson, the lexicographer and moralist, with remarks. Read before the Harveian Society. [*London Journal of Medicine*, vol. 1, 1849, pp. 615-623].

Stanhope, Philip Dormer, *Earl of Chesterfield.*—Two Dialogues ; containing a comparative view of the lives, characters, and writings of Philip, the late Earl of Chesterfield, and Dr. S. Johnson. London, 1787, 8vo.

Stephen, Leslie.—Samuel Johnson. (*English Men of Letters Series.*) London, 1878, 8vo.

Taine, H.—Histoire de la Littérature Anglaise. 4 tom. Paris, 1864, 8vo.
  Samuel Johnson, tom. iii., pp. 336-345.

——History of English Literature. 4 vols. Edinburgh, 1874, 8vo.
  Samuel Johnson, vol. iii., pp. 316-324.

Testard, Henri.—Histoire de la Littérature Anglaise, etc. Paris, 1882, 8vo.
  Johnson, pp. 315-321.

Thackeray, William Makepeace.—The Works of W. M. Thackeray, 24 vols. London, 1869-1886, 8vo.
  Dr. Johnson and Goldsmith, a drawing, in vol. xxiii., p. 413. First published in the *North British Review* of Feb. 1864, in Dr. John Brown's article on Thackeray.

Towers, Joseph.—A Letter to Dr. S. Johnson, occasioned by his late political publications. With an appendix containing some observations on a pamphlet ("An answer to the queries contained in a letter to Dr. Shebbeare, printed in the Public Ledger, Aug. 10 "), lately published by Dr. Shebbeare. [By J. Towers.] London, 1775, 8vo.

——An Essay on the Life, Character, and Writings of Dr. S Johnson. London, 1786, 8vo.
  There was an edition of this work issued in 1786, which is an exact duplicate in every respect but the title-page.

Thrale, [afterwards Piozzi], Mrs. H. L.—Anecdotes of S. Johnson during the last twenty years of his life. London, 1786, 8vo.
  There are several editions of this work.

——Autobiography, Letters, and Literary Remains of Mrs. Piozzi (Thrale). Edited, with notes,

and an introductory account of her life and writings by A. Hayward. 2 vols. London, 1861, 8vo.
——Second edition. London, 1861, 8vo.
Turner, Daniel. — Devotional Poetry Vindicated, in some remarks on the late Samuel Johnson's animadversions upon that subject in his Life of Waller, etc. Oxford [1785], 8vo.
Tyers, Thomas.—A biographical sketch of Dr. S. Johnson. [London, 1785 ?] 8vo.
Waller, John Francis.—Boswell and Johnson ; their companions and contemporaries. London [1881], 8vo.
Part of " Cassell's Monthly Shilling Library."
Ward, Thomas H.—The English Poets, etc. London, 1884, 8vo.
Samuel Johnson, by W. J. Courthope, vol. iii., pp. 245-253.
Webster, Noah.—A Letter to Dr. David Ramsay, of Charleston (S.C.), respecting the errors in Johnson's Dictionary. New-Haven, 1807, 12mo.
Welsh, Alfred H.—Development of English Literature and Language. 2 vols. Chicago, 1882, 8vo.
Samuel Johnson, vol. ii., pp. 172-178.
White, Thomas Holt.—A review of Johnson's criticism on the style of Milton's English Prose, etc. London, 1818, 8vo.
Whyte, Edward Athenry.—Remarks on Boswell's Life of Johnson, etc. Dublin, 1797, 8vo.
——S. and E. A.—A Miscellany, containing remarks on Boswell's Johnson, etc. Dublin, 1799, 8vo.

Whyte, S. and E A. — Another edition. Miscellanea Nova, etc. Dublin, 1800, 8vo.
——Another edition. Dublin, 1801, 8vo.
Wilks, Samuel C. — Christian Essays. 2 vols. London, 1817, 8vo.
Johnson comprises pp. 236-266, vol. i., of the essay, *True and false repose in death.*
Wrangham, Francis.—The British Plutarch, containing the Lives of the most eminent divines, etc. A new edition. 6 vols. London, 1816, 8vo.
Dr. Samuel Johnson, vol. vi., pp. 301-362.
Yonge, Charles Duke. — Three Centuries of English Literature. London, 1872, 8vo.
Johnson, A.D. 1709-1784, pp. 389-406.

MAGAZINE ARTICLES.

Johnson, Dr. Samuel.—General Magazine, 1789, pp. 405-410. Evangelical Review, by S. A. Allibone, vol. 17, pp. 502, etc. —Harper's New Monthly Magazine, by T. B. Macaulay, vol. 14, 1857, pp. 41-497 ; reprinted from the Encyclopædia Britannica ; same article, Littell's Living Age, vol. 53, 1857, pp. 1-19.—British Quarterly, by J. Dennis, vol. 70, 1879, pp. 347-371 ; same article, Littell's Living Age. vol. 144, 1880, pp. 259-272.—Contemporary Review, by A. Birrell, vol. 47, 1885, pp. 25-39. — New Monthly Magazine, vol. 3, N.S., 1873, pp. 376-384 and 432-440. Littell's Living Age, by G. D., vol. 52, 1857, pp. 742-750 ; vol. 60, 1859, pp. 353-360.—National Magazine, vol. 1, pp. 393, etc.,

Johnson, Dr. Samuel.
488 etc. ; vol. 2, pp. 9, etc., 488 etc.—Leisure Hour. 1852, pp. 737-742.—Fortnightly Review, by Edmund Gosse, vol. 36, N.S., 1884, pp. 780-786.—Christian World Magazine, by J. Ewing Ritchie, vol. 13, 1877, pp. 824-833. — Antiquarian Magazine, by E. Walford, vol. 6, 1884, pp. 259-263.

——*and Bishop Warburton.* Blackwood's Edinburgh Magazine, by C. R., vol. 8, 1820, pp. 243-252.

——*and Carlyle : Common Sense versus Transcendentalism.* National Review, by W. J. Courthope, vol. 2, 1883, pp. 317-332.

——*and David Hume.* Blackwood's Edinburgh Magazine, vol. 3, 1818, pp. 511-513.

——*and Dr. Hookwell.* Quarterly Review, vol. 87, 1850, pp. 59-63 ; same article, Littell's Living Age, vol. 26, 1850, pp. 337-341.

——*and Garrick.* North American Review, vol. 4, 1826, pp. 38-47.

——*and Hannah More.* Chambers's Edinburgh Journal, vol. 15, N.S., 1851, pp. 380-382.

——*and his Age.* Quarterly Review, vol. 159, 1885, pp. 147-174.

——*et ses Critiques.* Revue des Deux Mondes, by Léon Boucher, tom. 37, 1880, pp. 674-697.

——*and his Wife, Macaulay on.* Cornhill Magazine, by G. B. H., vol. 42, 1880, pp. 573-581; same article, Littell's Living Age, vol. 147, 1880, pp. 627-633.

——*and Mrs. Piozzi.* Belgravia, by Percy Fitzgerald, vol. 15, 1871, pp. 183-196.

Johnson, Dr. Samuel.
——*and Mrs. Thrale.* St. James's Magazine, vol. 1, 1861, pp. 243-248.

——*and Oliver Goldsmith.* De Bow's Review, vol. 28, 1860, pp. 504-513.

——*and Savage.* Chambers's Edinburgh Journal, by Robert Chambers, 1847, pp. 65-68.

——*and Sir Joshua Reynolds.* Month, vol. 3, 1865, pp. 403-410.

——*and the Fleet Street Taverns.* Gentlemen's Magazine, by Percy Fitzgerald, 1881, pp. 305-317.

——*Anecdotes of.* Democratic Review, vol. 11, N.S., 1842, pp. 164-170.

——*as a Temperance Moralist.* Meliora, vol. 8, 1865, pp. 60-77

——*as Christian and Critic.* Eclectic Review, vol. 9, N.S., 1855, pp. 153-168 ; same article, Eclectic Magazine, vol. 34, 1855, pp. 492-500, and Littell's Living Age, vol. 45, 1855, pp. 221-227.

——*At Lichfield.* [Illustrated.] The Antiquary, by H. B. Wheatley, vol. 10, 1884, pp. 233-239.

——*Biographers and Critics of.* Westminster Review, vol. 55, N.S., 1879, pp. 1-39 ; same article, Appleton's Journal of Literature, vol. 6, N.S., 1879, pp. 308-325.

——*Boswell's Letters on.* Christian Observer, vol. 59, 1859, pp. 9-21.

——*Boswell's Life and Conversations of, condensed by Alex. Main.* Nation, by J. R. Dennett, vol. 18, 1874, pp. 253, 254.

——*Boswell's Life of.* (*Croker's Edition.*) North American Review, by W. B. O. Peabody, vol.

CHRONOLOGICAL LIST OF WORKS.

Printed by WALTER SCOTT, *Felling, Newcastle-on-Tyne.*